The Ghost of
the Stanley Cup

Roy MacGregor

An M&S Paperback Original from
McClelland & Stewart Ltd.
The Canadian Publishers

The author is grateful to Doug Gibson, who thought up this series, and to Alex Schultz, who pulls it off.

An M&S Paperback Original from
McClelland & Stewart Ltd.

Library and Archives Canada Cataloguing in Publication

MacGregor, Roy, 1948–
    The ghost of the Stanley Cup

(The Screech Owls series; 11)
"An M&S paperback".
ISBN 0-7710-5622-2

I. Title.   II. Series: MacGregor, Roy, 1948–   .
Screech Owls series; 11.

PS8575.G84G46 1999   jC813'.54   C99-932607-4
PZ7.M34Gh 1999

We acknowledge the financial support of the Government of Canada through the Book Publishing Industry Development Program and that of the Government of Ontario through the Ontario Media Development Corporation's Ontario Book Initiative. We further acknowledge the support of the Canada Council for the Arts and the Ontario Arts Council for our publishing program.

Cover illustration by Gregory C. Banning
Typeset in Bembo by M&S, Toronto

Printed and bound in Canada

McClelland & Stewart Ltd.
The Canadian Publishers
481 University Avenue
Toronto, Ontario
M5G 2E9
www.mcclelland.com

4 5 6 7 8   09 08 07 06 05

For the Boys – Dave Rider, Alan (Lyle) Siew, Stan Thomson, Dustin Record, and Homayoun Chaudry – who were on their way home the night of June 27, 1999.

Never to be forgotten by family and friends, schoolmates and teammates. The Screech Owls thank them for inspiration, and dedicate the neverending season to their memory.

NISH WAS DEAD!

One moment he was screaming "*I'M GONNA HURL!*" from the seat behind Travis Lindsay – who was desperately hanging on to the bucking, slamming, sliding monster beneath them – the next he was airborne, a chubby twelve-year-old in a red crash helmet, a black rubber wetsuit, and a yellow life jacket, spinning high over the rest of the Screech Owls and smack into the churning whirlpool at the bottom of the most dangerous chute of the long rapids.

Nish entered his watery grave without a sound, the splash instantly erased by the rushing, tea-coloured water of the mighty Ottawa River as it choked itself through the narrow canyon of wet, dripping rock and roared triumphantly out the other end. Screaming and spinning one second, he was gone the next – his teammates so terrified they could do nothing but tighten their iron-locked grips on their paddles and the rope of the river raft.

Nish was dead!

Travis closed his eyes to the slap of cold water as it cuffed off the dripping rock walls and spilled in over his face. *Would any of them get out alive? Would it be up to him, as team captain and best friend, to tell Nish's mother?*

"Did my little Wayne have any last words?" poor sweet Mrs. Nishikawa would ask.

"Yes," Travis would have to answer.

"What were they?" Mrs. Nishikawa would say, a Kleenex held to her trusting eyes.

And Travis would have to tell her: "*'I'm gonna hurl.'*"

The Screech Owls had come to Ottawa for a special edition of the Little Stanley Cup. Instead of in January or February, it was being held over the Canada Day long weekend and was going to honour the one hundredth anniversary of the Ottawa Silver Seven – hockey's very first Stanley Cup dynasty. It was to be a peewee hockey tournament the likes of which had never been seen before. The Hockey Hall of Fame in Toronto was bringing up the original Stanley Cup that Governor General Lord Stanley had given to the people of Canada in 1893, there was going to be a special display of hockey memorabilia from the early 1900s, and the Governor General herself was going to present the cup to the winning team. The Sports Network was going to televise the final, and special rings – "*Stanley Cup rings!*"

Nish had shouted when he heard – would be awarded to the champions.

But it was unlike other tournaments for more reasons than that. Muck Munro, who always said he had little use for summer hockey, wasn't there to coach. Muck had told them he couldn't get off work, but the Owls figured he hadn't tried all that hard. If Muck took a summer holiday, he preferred to head into the bush for a week of trout fishing. Muck's two assistants, Barry and Ty, hadn't been able to get away either. The team was essentially under the control of good old Mr. Dillinger, who was wonderful at sharpening skates but didn't know much about breakout patterns, and Larry Ulmar – Data – who was great at cheering but not much for strategy. Right now, Data was waiting for the Owls at the end of the ride, deeply disappointed that the river guides hadn't been able to figure out a way to strap his wheelchair into the big, bucking rafts.

Nor were the Screech Owls staying with local families for this tournament. Instead, they were camping, along with most of the other teams, at a church camp farther down the river, within sight of the highrises of Ottawa. It was an ideal location, and the tournament games were deliberately spaced out to allow for day trips. The teams were booked to go river rafting, mountain biking in the Gatineau Hills, and even off to world-famous Algonquin Park, where they hoped to see

3

moose and bear. The tournament final itself was to be played in the Corel Centre, where the Ottawa Senators had played only the winter before. Nish had said it was only proper that he win his first Stanley Cup ring on a rink where NHL stars had skated.

But now Nish was lost overboard, bouncing, spinning, bumping along the bottom of the Ottawa River, snapping turtles pulling at his desperately clutching fingers, leeches already sucking out his blood.

It had been the guide's suggestion that one of them join him at the back of the raft and help steer. Nish, of course, had jumped up first with both hands raised and shouted out that the seat was his. The new player, Samantha Bennett, had also raised her hand to volunteer, and Travis was quick to notice a small flash of anger in Sam's green eyes when the guide gave in and picked Nish. Sam, who'd only moved to Tamarack two months earlier, was Data's replacement on defence. Big and strong, she was as competitive off the ice as on, and almost as loud and just possibly as funny as Nish himself. Andy Higgins had even started calling her "Nish-*ette*," though never to her face. Nish, to her, was a rival as top Screech Owls' defender, not an example for her to copy.

The waters had been calm when Nish went back to sit with the guide. Once, Travis thought he had seen Nish unbuckle his safety harness while the real guide – "Call me Hughie" – pointed out the sights along the river. Travis hadn't worried about Nish's harness until, around the next bend in the river, his ears were filled with a frightening roar, and the water, now rushing, loomed white and foaming ahead of them.

It hadn't seemed possible to Travis that a rubber raft could chance such a run. What if it was punctured on the rocks? But the guide had sent them straight into the highest boils of the current, and the huge raft had folded and sprung and tossed several of them out of their seats as it slid and jumped and smashed through the water. They turned abruptly at the bottom and rammed head-on into a rooster tail of rolling water, the rush now flinging them backwards as if shot from a catapult.

Nish had held on fine through all that – despite his undone safety harness.

Down the river they went, the water roaring and thundering between tight rocks as the runs grew more and more intense. But always the big raft came through, the Screech Owls screaming happily and catching their breath each time they made it down a fast run and shot out the other side into calmer, deeper waters.

But this last time had been too much. The big raft slid into the channel, snaking over the rises, and up ahead Nish saw Lars Johanssen, Wilson Kelly, and Sarah Cuthbertson being bounced right out of their seats. But they had their hands looped carefully around the rope, as instructed, and fortunately they came right back down.

Travis had also left his seat, the quick feeling of weightlessness both exhilarating and alarming. He held tight and bounced back down, hard, and was instantly into the next rise.

That was when he heard his great friend's famous last words – "*I'M GONNA HURL!*" – and the next moment he was watching, helpless, as Nish slipped into that horrifying watery grave.

Nish, lost overboard.

Drowned.

His body never to be recovered.

2

"*KA-WA-BUN-GA!*"

Travis spun so fast in his seat he almost turned right around. But then he realized the raft was also turning. They'd reached the bottom of the run. The water was slowing, circling back in small eddies and swirls. Hughie, laughing and digging in hard with his steering paddles to follow the flow, was pointing back up the water.

"*KA-WA-BUN-GA!*"

It was Nish! He was lying flat on his back as if the chute were a La-Z-Boy and he was casually watching television, not magically returning from the dead. His chubby hands were folded behind his head for a pillow, and the life jacket had him riding high as a cork as he came down, feet first, and spun into the small whirlpool at the bottom before bumping gently into the raft filled with astonished, delighted Screech Owls.

"*Can we do that again?*" he shouted to the guide.

Hughie laughed so hard Travis thought he might fall in too.

"*Get in here!*" Hughie said, and with some difficulty hauled Nish up over the side.

"CHUCK HIM BACK IN!" a loud voice shouted from the front of the raft. "WHALES ARE OUT OF SEASON!"

It was Sam. The Screech Owls – with one exception – roared with laughter. Nish rolled on his side and spat a mouthful of river water in Sam's direction. Travis caught sight of his friend's face. It was burning so bright it almost turned the water on his cheeks to steam.

Hughie, still laughing, helped Nish back into his seat and, this time, tied him to the raft. They continued downriver, flowing with the current and shooting fast through the narrows. Several times riders flew into the air and bounced on the thick sides of the raft, but they all held tight to the ropes and, when necessary, to each other. Despite Nish's recommendation, no one wanted to shoot a rapids without the raft under them.

It was a wonderful way to spend a day. The river seemed designed for rafting, with long, luxurious drifts between the white-water chutes and, around noon, a rocky river island suddenly looming before them with a calm, sheltered landing area downriver and a large, flat, rocky surface for lunch by the shore.

Hughie broke out two large coolers that had been secured by Velcro straps at the centre of the raft. Several Owls helped him haul them over to a flat rock where several wooden blocks were scattered around a black and damp-looking fire pit. The thick cedar blocks made perfect stools, and several of the Owls shed their helmets and life jackets and sat down to watch the guide work.

Inside one cooler was paper and dry wood, pots and pans and cooking oil, and tin cups and paper plates and towels. Inside the other was food: hot dogs and buns, boxes of Kraft Dinner, Kool-Aid, tins of cookies, and several thick bundles wrapped in tinfoil which, when carefully folded back by the guide, revealed the pink flesh of lake trout. "Caught 'em myself," Hughie bragged.

He began to set the fire, carefully crumpling up the paper, then building a thatch of thinly sliced kindling on top before striking a match. The fire caught quickly and he began feeding it, first with the dry dead branches of a nearby spruce, then with split birch that had been piled there earlier, presumably by the rafting company.

"Go explore the island while I get things ready," Hughie suggested. "Just make sure you have your life jackets on."

The Screech Owls began walking about the small island. It was hot in the sun with the wet-suits and bulky jackets on, and Travis could feel his skin prickling with sweat. If he felt uncomfortable, he thought, how must Nish feel?

But if Nish was bothered by the heat, he didn't show it. He was up ahead and in full voice, surrounded by his friends on the team – Wilson, Andy, Lars, Fahd Noorizadeh, Derek Dillinger, Gordie Griffith, Jeremy Weathers, and Jesse Highboy. Slightly ahead of them, Sarah was walking with Sam, Liz Moscovitz, and Jenny Staples. Travis could see Sam whispering and the other girls giggling.

"I coulda died back there," Nish was saying just a bit too loudly.

"I thought you *were* dead," said Fahd.

"Just lucky for them it was me who flew off," Nish boasted. "Good thing for them I'm such a strong swimmer."

Sarah couldn't resist. She turned, her face questioning: "You looked like you were 'floating,' not swimming."

Nish dismissed her with a wave of his hand. "I had to get clear of the bottom first. You wouldn't believe what it's like down there. Just look at how hard that water's going" – he pointed to the wildest section of the river as it pounded and churned and roared through the narrow stretch between island and shore – "Nobody'd survive that if they weren't a strong swimmer like me."

"I wouldn't," agreed Fahd.

Travis wasn't so sure. It seemed to him that the wetsuit and life jacket may have done all the work, that Nish was merely along for the ride from the moment he splashed in. But he supposed if Nish wanted to make himself out to be a hero, he'd let him. After all, it had happened a million times before.

"HEY – HUGHIE!"

It was Sam's big voice again, calling over the roar of the river. The guide stepped back from his blazing campfire and looked over to where Sam and most of the other Owls were standing.

They were right below the high bluff that formed the upstream end of the island. It was like a miniature mountain, with a small pine tree hanging on valiantly to the side.

"OKAY IF WE CLIMB UP?"

"*I'll have to come up with you!*" he called. He threw more wood on the fire. It would be a while before there were coals enough for cooking.

Sam was already scrambling up. There seemed to be a series of hand- and foot-holds all the way to the top, and her hands and feet moved deftly from grip to grip. She was halfway up by the time the guide made it over to them.

"*Slow down up there!*" Hughie called after her. But he didn't seem angry. He took a run and leaped to the first grip himself, moving up surely and quickly, as if he knew the face of the bluff by heart. Dmitri Yakushev, Sarah, Simon Milliken, and Jesse were right behind him.

"Let's go!" Travis said to Nish.

"Ah, who wants to do something stupid like that?" Nish said.

But Travis wasn't listening. He was hurrying to join the scramble up to the top. The view from up there would be fantastic. With the thick mist rising off the river as it roared by on both sides of the island, the top was barely visible. Once up there, it would probably feel as if they were floating on a cloud.

Travis joined in with Andy and Jenny and Willie Granger, who were about to start climbing.

Andy looked at Travis, puzzled. "Isn't Nish coming?"

"Sure," Travis said as he turned – only to realize Nish hadn't come with him.

Of course – Nish was terrified of heights!

"What's wrong with him?" demanded Andy.

Andy hadn't been with them at Lake Placid, when Nish had freaked out on the drive up White Mountain. He'd panicked again at the CN Tower in Toronto, but Andy was new to the team then and probably hadn't noticed. The truth was that Nish – big brave Nish – had one remarkable weak spot: he could not bear heights.

"C'mon, Nish!" Travis shouted encouragingly. "It's not so high."

Too many of the Owls were watching for Nish to ignore the challenge. He swaggered over, but Travis noticed that Nish's high colour from his fall overboard had vanished. He was growing whiter by the moment – almost as if the blood were draining straight out the bottom of his wetsuit.

"Get going, then," Nish ordered. "I'm right behind you."

The others scrambled up with Travis at the rear. It was hard work, but relatively easy climbing. The route had been well established. Travis reached the first ledge and paused to catch his breath. He looked back. Nish, barely two metres off the ground, was staring up helplessly, his face pale and frightened. He looked on the verge of tears and was breathing heavily.

Travis gave his friend an easy way out. "You're probably beat from the spill," he said.

Nish nodded gratefully. "Yeah, I think you're right. I'll maybe just hang back a minute and catch my breath."

"See you up there," Travis said, knowing he wouldn't.

Travis hurried to catch up. He soon settled into a rhythm, finding a handgrip whenever needed, a foot-hold at just the right distance, roots and rock edges and branches perfectly placed for reaching out to and pulling yourself up. It was fun, and he moved quickly.

When Travis looked over the top of the rock face, he saw the Owls already there, gathered around Hughie. He was pointing out the far Gatineau Hills.

It was a beautiful place to stand. The rocks were stark and wet with the mist that rose like steam all about them. It seemed they were in a dream world, walking among the clouds, able to fly if they wished.

"Anybody ever fall off?" Sam was asking, her green eyes flashing with excitement. Now that they were in the sun, her red hair sparkled wildly with the mist settling on it from below.

"You'd die," pronounced Fahd with his usual air of disaster.

"Nah," laughed Hughie. "The water's forty feet deep on this side. You couldn't touch bottom if you tried; you'd be swept away downstream before you'd gone three metres deep."

"Anybody ever jump?" Sam asked.

"You nuts?" Fahd said.

"Sometimes," said Hughie. "There's a few guides who'll do it. We once had a television crew here filming it for *Extreme Sports*."

"Did you jump?" asked Jesse.

"I'm not that crazy," laughed Hughie.

"Well," said Sam, "*I* am!"

And with that she turned and raced for the edge, springing once on both feet high out over the gorge then tucking her legs into her body in a full somersault.

"*Hey!*" shouted the guide.

They all raced towards the empty space where a half-second earlier Sam had stood. Travis reached the edge just in time to see her disappear down through the mist and into the churning, boiling river.

"SHE'LL DROWN!" screeched Jenny.

"She can't," said Hughie, gathering himself. "She's fully outfitted. She'll be all right."

The Screech Owls stood leaning over the edge, all of them staring into the hump of rolling water where Sam had disappeared.

"She won't come up there," said the guide. "Watch for her downstream."

The Screech Owls stared down towards the calmer water where they'd drawn the raft up onto the rocks.

They saw Nish first. He was standing alone down by the raft, looking completely lost, trying to stay out of sight of the others.

And now they were all staring at him.

"What's Nish doing there?" Fahd asked, although it was all too obvious.

"*There she comes!*" called Hughie, pointing.

They followed his finger. Travis noticed the red crash helmet first, then the bright yellow life jacket. Then the fist, pumping the air as if she'd just scored the winning goal in the Little Stanley Cup.

"*KA-WA-BUN-GA!*"

Nish's call, but clearly not his voice.

It was Sam, pumping her fist and hollering at Nish.

"*KA-WA-BUN-GA! CHICKEN BOY!*"

Sam was swimming, strong and easily, towards the shallows where the raft was docked. She kept pumping her fist.

"*KA-WA-BUN-GA!*"

Travis could see Nish look up at them, his face filled with the painful knowledge that he had just been humiliated. Now they all knew he had chickened out of the climb. And now they all knew there had been nothing particularly brave or talented about his overboard ride down the river.

Nish had just been out–Nished by Sam.

He was a long way away, and there was heavy mist in the air, but Travis didn't need to see Nish's face clearly to be able to read it.

Total fury.

3

"I'LL GET HER BACK – DON'T YOU WORRY."

Nish might have been talking to himself. He was flat on his back, wearing only his boxer shorts, his sleeping bag kicked off to the side and his pillow covered with candy wrappers: Tootsie Roll, Mars Bar, Mr. Big, Milky Way. In Nish's opinion, a four-course meal.

The boys had woken early. There was so much going on during the Little Stanley Cup, it seemed there was no time left for sleeping. They'd been up until midnight watching the Canada Day fireworks on Parliament Hill – the greatest display of brilliant colour and raw *noise* that Travis had ever experienced – and this morning they had been roused at 7:30 to get ready for their first practice. It was, for the Screech Owls, even better than a game, for they were going to skate on the Corel Centre ice and use the same dressing room as the Ottawa Senators.

Travis lay in the big, army-style tent, half-listening to Nish ramble on about getting his revenge on Sam, and half-watching the sunlight play over the tent. The light seemed to pour through a thousand pinpricks in the canvas – yet it had rained during the night and they'd remained warm and dry.

"But how?" Andy finally asked Nish.

Travis winced. The worst mistake you could make with Nish was to lead him on. The others in the tent – Fahd, Jesse, Lars, and Dmitri – knew it too, but Andy had been unable to resist.

"I'm not sure yet," Nish answered, then giggled softly to himself. "But it'll be good, *real* good, I promise you that."

Travis closed his eyes, not even daring to imagine what schemes were racing through his best friend's twisted little brain.

The sun was now so strong on the tent, it seemed Travis's eyelids had been spray-painted red from the inside.

It was already getting too hot – he could hardly wait to hit the ice.

Travis could never quite understand what Muck had against summer hockey. Muck always said summer was for other sports – baseball to improve your eye-hand co-ordination, soccer to help your footwork and passing, biking for conditioning – and claimed that the reason so many kids dropped out of hockey in their teenage years was that they were sick and tired of playing the game twelve months of the year. Perhaps Travis would one day agree with his coach, but not now.

He loved the way everything about summer hockey was backwards. In winter you came in to the warmth and shed bulky outdoor clothes; in summer you came in to the cool and put on bulky equipment. Travis liked the dressing up instead of dressing down. He liked that first step onto a fresh ice surface when he could kick once and just glide freely. He often thought that the first turn around the rink in summer must be as close as a kid can come to feeling like an astronaut stepping outside the spaceship: so heavily insulated, head helmeted, gravity and friction defied, his body drifting and soaring with the slightest effort.

Even better, the Owls were in a rink where NHL players had performed. Here, on this very ice surface, was where Alexei Yashin and Daniel Alfredsson and Marian Hossa had starred for the Senators. Here was where Jaromir Jagr had scored, where Patrick Roy and Dominik Hasek had kicked out the shots. And here, he suddenly remembered, was where Wayne Gretzky had played his final game ever in Canada. Because of that, it was a rink that belonged to Canadian history.

Mr. Dillinger was doing the best he could. He set out pylons and dumped a bucket of pucks, and he tried to talk like Muck and outline plays like Ty, but it wasn't the same. Poor Mr. Dillinger, sweat beading on his bald head, could barely skate. He needed his stick on the ice for support, and when he tried to fire a puck into a corner so the power play could work on their cycling, he fell over onto one knee.

"*Need some help out there?*" a voice called from behind the bench.

Mr. Dillinger stood up, knocked the snow off his leg and stared over, not sure whether he was being laughed at or not.

A handsome young man was standing beside Data, who had pulled his chair up to the bench and was following the practice with a playboard on his lap. The man had short dark hair and was smiling – a nice smile, an inviting smile. He was holding up his skates, tied together at the laces, as if to suggest he be asked out on the ice.

Mr. Dillinger skated over, stopping so awkwardly he threw his big hip into the boards and sprung open the bench gate. He almost fell, catching himself at the last moment.

"What makes you think we need help?" Mr. Dillinger said, with as much dignity as he could muster.

The young man smiled again – his teeth flashing under the strong lights of the Corel

Centre – and Mr. Dillinger was instantly smiling back, then laughing at himself.

"I'm Joe Hall," the young man said, holding out his hand.

4

"GLAD TO MEET YOU, JOE HALL," MR. DILLINGER said, taking off his hockey glove and reaching for the young man's hand. Mr. Dillinger's hand seemed to disappear into Joe Hall's like a gopher into a large hole.

"I live down by the campsite – heard some of the other coaches saying your coach couldn't make the trip. True?"

Mr. Dillinger was nodding, catching his breath. "I'm just the manager and skate sharpener. Data here's more of a coach than I am."

Joe Hall turned his beaming smile on Data. "I can see that," he said. "You've got some drills worked out on that board, I see."

Data seemed shocked, instantly shy. "Oh, I was just fooling around."

"Nah, they're good," protested Joe Hall. He turned his gaze back on Mr. Dillinger. "I'd be honoured to help you run the practice. Just say the word."

Mr. Dillinger nodded gratefully. He looped off Muck's whistle and tossed it to Joe Hall, who slipped it around his thick neck and sat down on the bench to put his skates on. A stick and gloves lay behind him. He'd come prepared.

"Just what we need," Nish whispered into the back of Travis's helmet. "Another *expert*."

Travis turned, irritated. "We need *somebody* who knows what he's doing."

"I think he's kind of cute," said Sam.

"So do I," agreed Sarah.

"Better than anything else we've seen around here, that's for sure," added Sam.

"*Get a life!*" Nish practically spat in her direction.

Sam rolled her eyes. Sarah giggled. Usually it was Sarah who took the shots at Nish and kept him in line. She seemed happy to be sharing her duties.

Joe Hall was ready in less than a minute. He stepped out onto the ice surface and flexed, stretching carefully before looping around the rink a couple of times. It seemed to Travis that Joe Hall hadn't been on skates for some time, but he could see that, even on rusty legs, he had a marvellous, powerful stride.

"Okay, Owls," Joe Hall said when the team had gathered around. "Let's have us a practice."

Twenty minutes later, Travis was bent over double, sucking for wind. Nish, splayed out flat in the corner, was groaning and gasping for air. Andy was hanging over the boards, gulping his breaths. Everywhere it was the same, with one — no, two — exceptions. Sarah, who seemed to find skating easier than breathing, was still flying about the ice in her lovely, effortless stride. And right behind her, a little less elegant but more powerful, was Sam. They were laughing.

Joe Hall was a taskmaster. He skated them until most of the Owls had either dropped or were about to drop. He ran complicated breakout drills that sent the puck flying out to centre ice so quickly that Sarah, waiting for the pass, barely had to flick it on her backhand to send the swift Dmitri in on clear breakaways. He had them working the corners, practising penalty-killing and switching, on a rap of his stick, from zone to man-on-man coverage. It was exhausting, but it was a superb, hard practice. Muck would have approved.

Joe Hall blew hard on the whistle, calling the players down into a far corner. He had them drop to one knee when they arrived. Nish arrived on both knees, spinning wildly, and knocked into Andy and Fahd and Lars so hard he sent them tumbling like bowling pins.

Joe Hall waited until everything was absolutely silent, then he stared at Nish and spoke in a low, steady voice. "You can go and sit on the bench, mister. We've still got some business to do here."

Nish looked stunned. He turned, mouth open, and Travis could see the pink spreading across his cheeks. But no one was offering any sympathy.

"Get going," Joe Hall said. "You're wasting our ice time."

Nish rose to his skates. Slowly he skated away, the rasp of his skates uncannily loud in the empty rink. Not a single Screech Owl even dared to breathe.

But Joe Hall was smiling again. He had forgotten already about Wayne Nishikawa, trouble-maker. "Anyone here know about the Silver Seven?" he asked.

"Data would," Sarah said.

"They were hockey's first dynasty," offered Fahd.

"That's correct," said Joe Hall, nodding. "They were the original Ottawa Senators. Four Stanley Cups in a row at the start of this last century. Not even Gretzky's Edmonton Oilers managed that. Guys like Harry 'Rat' Westwick, 'Bones' Allen, 'Peerless' Percy LeSueur, and 'One-Eyed' Frank McGee."

The players giggled at the names.

"You don't hear nicknames like that these days, do you?" Joe Hall said. "The kid I just sent off, what's his name?"

"Wayne Nishikawa," Fahd offered.

"And his nickname?"

"Nish."

Joe Hall shrugged. "Figures. There's no imagi-nation in hockey any more. All you kids should have nicknames – they're as important in this game as numbers. What *should* be Nish's nickname?"

" 'Chicken'?" suggested a voice from the back. It was Sam.

The other players giggled. Joe Hall looked from face to face, waiting for an explanation, but no one was volunteering.

"Did you have one?" Fahd asked.

"Me? Yeah, I did."

"What was it?"

Joe Hall shook his head: "You'll have to figure that one out for yourself."

"No fair!" protested Fahd. But Joe Hall was already changing topic.

"Let me tell you something about 'One-Eyed' Frank and Harry the 'Rat,' " he said. "They're both in the Hockey Hall of Fame, you know."

"We were there!" said Jenny.

"Then you should know *why* they're in the Hall of Fame. The 'Rat' was one of the best skaters who ever played the game. If you really had to have a goal, you counted on him. Frank McGee once scored fourteen goals in a single Stanley Cup game – a record no one's ever going to break. How do you think they scored those goals?"

Fahd raised his hand like he was in class. Joe Hall nodded at him.

"Breakaways," he suggested.

Joe Hall shook his head. "How do you get a breakaway?" he asked Fahd.

"You fire the puck up to someone who's breaking."

Joe Hall smiled and pointed. "Exactly! But what if you couldn't do that?"

"You mean offside?" asked Andy.

"No," said Joe Hall. "I mean what if the rules didn't allow you – or anyone for that matter – to pass a puck *up* to a teammate?"

"What kind of a rule is that?" asked Lars.

"It was the rule they played under. It wasn't until 1929 that hockey brought in the forward pass. Did anyone know that?"

"No," Fahd answered for them all.

"For more than thirty years they played the game by using only drop passes and back passes – and still 'One-Eyed' Frank McGee was able to score fourteen goals in one game. It worked for the Silver Seven, don't you think?"

"I guess," said Fahd.

"I guess so too," said Joe Hall. "And so we're going to bring that pass back to this tournament. We're going to move ahead by going backwards."

For more than thirty minutes, Joe Hall had the Owls work on drop passes and back passes. He had them scrimmage with one new rule added – no forward passes. At first it confused the players terribly, but after a while they started to get the hang of it and began moving up the ice in waves, with each successive wave rushing quicker just as pucks were dropped back to them.

"We look like Russians!" shouted Dmitri proudly.

"We look like idiots!" corrected Nish, who had been allowed back into the play.

But Travis didn't think so. There was method to Joe Hall's madness, and the Owls were starting to look for the play developing behind them. They were using themselves as decoys, drawing off checks while leaving pucks for teammates rushing up behind. It might not have looked quite right, but it was working.

Sarah looped behind her own net and, with a burst of speed, slipped straight up centre, sending the opposing defence – Nish paired with Lars this time – backpedalling wildly. She dropped the puck neatly to Sam, charging up from her defensive position.

Travis could see the play. Sarah had used her body to "accidentally" brush Lars back and take him out of the play. It was just Sam on Nish, with Travis coming up fast.

If Sam could drop to Travis, he would have a clear shot on Jeremy, who was already shimmying backwards into his net, glove ready.

Sam saw the play, too. She dropped the puck deftly between her skates and turned to see if Travis was in his expected position.

And that's exactly when Nish "smoked" her.

The sound was astonishing. It was more like a collision in the parking lot than a hit just inside the blueline. There was the sound of air bursting from lungs, pads giving, plastic cracking, sticks and skates and bodies colliding.

Sam went down hard, sprawling toward the corner.

Nish, who barely kept upright, staggered once, then dropped his stick and gloves.

He tucked his hands under his armpits, dropped into a crouch, and began skating in a wide circle past the fallen Sam.

"CLUCK! CLUCK–CLUCK–CLUCK!" Nish cackled as he looped around the ice in an exaggerated chicken dance. "CLUCK! CLUCK–CLUCK–CLUCK–CLUCK–CLUCK!"

Joe Hall's whistle sounded like the scream that had never come from Sam. Travis had often wondered how Muck could put so much emotion into his whistle – shrill for anger, slow and rolling for contentment – but this was a new sound, a frightening one.

Nish stopped his stupid show. Joe Hall came skating back, pointing, his hand shaking.

"You're outta here, Mister! The dressing room – and make it fast!"

Nish didn't argue. He left his stick and gloves on the ice and never even broke stride as he leapt through the gate leading to the dressing room.

Travis turned his attention back to Sam. She was on her knees, fighting for wind. Sarah was already there, an arm over Sam's shoulders.

Sam gathered her breath, put her skate down, and stood, a bit unsteadily.

She was laughing!

5

THE SCREECH OWLS PLAYED THEIR FIRST GAME against the Rideau Rebels at the Kanata Recreation Centre, a double ice-surface rink within sight of the peach-coloured walls of the Corel Centre. It was almost as good, Mr. Dillinger said, because this was where the Senators practised when the Corel Centre was unavailable. There was even an elevator for Data to use to get down to the dressing-room level.

Data had struck up a fast friendship with Sam. She seemed to know almost as much about *Star Trek* as he did, and on the bus the two of them argued endlessly about which was superior, *Star Trek* (Data's choice) or *Star Wars* (Sam's choice). The day after practice, when Sam stood outside the bus, heavy equipment bag slung over her shoulder, and shouted up to Mr. Dillinger "*HIjol!*" – Klingon for "Beam me up!" – she won Data's heart forever.

Nish seemed unwilling to take any competition from Sam for the spotlight. On the night the Owls had a team dinner at the camp with the tournament organizers, it looked as if he was going to behave himself, until the visiting church minister suggested that, instead of a prayer before the meal, they go around the tables and tell the gathering one special thing in their lives for which they were particularly grateful.

"My grandparents," said Travis.

"My country," said Lars, who was fiercely proud of being from Sweden.

"My new friend and teammate, Data," said Sam.

"Mail-order catalogues," said Nish.

The minister, already moving his finger on to the next Owl, jumped back, his attention returning to Nish, a puzzled expression on his face.

"Why, son?"

Nish grinned. "I'm grateful for the lingerie ads."

The girls on the team all groaned. Lars and Andy started giggling and couldn't stop, finally ducking down and hiding underneath the table-cloth until Mr. Dillinger, his own face flushed red, went over and shooed them out. Travis looked over at Sarah, who rolled her eyes and spun a finger beside her right temple. Travis just nodded back. Good thing for Nish that Joe Hall hadn't been able to make the dinner.

Travis thought he understood Nish's bizarre behaviour, but Joe Hall was a puzzle. He seemed to be around, much of the time – then suddenly gone. They asked him where he lived, and he pointed up the river and said he had the first cottage on the shore around the point. But some of the Owls had gone hiking that way, and they had seen nothing. They asked him what level he'd played at – he had clearly been a superior hockey player – and all he'd said was "high."

"Why'd you quit?" Fahd wanted to know. "Injury?"

That's what Travis had figured. That's what had happened to Muck, who still limped from the bad break that had ended his junior career and ended, forever, his dreams of making the NHL. Joe Hall didn't limp, but it could have been something else. An eye? Concussion?

"No," he said. "No injury."

"Well, what then?" Fahd persisted.

Joe Hall stared at them a moment, as if unsure whether to tell them.

"I . . . ," he began. "I . . . just got sick, okay?"

Nothing more had been said. But it didn't stop the team from talking about Joe Hall among themselves. Lars was fascinated by Joe Hall's way of playing the game. "European," Lars called it. "Russian," Dmitri argued. But it was neither, Travis figured. It was *old* – like Joe Hall himself had said – the way "Rat" Westwick and "One-Eyed" Frank McGee used to play the game in this very city.

"Did you notice his stick?" Sarah had asked Travis after that first practice.

"No. What kind does he use?" Travis asked, thinking that's what Sarah meant: Sherwood, maybe, or Easton, or Titan, or Nike.

"The blade's completely straight," she said. "I couldn't tell whether it was right or left when I picked it up."

"*Straight?*"

"As a ruler."

Travis shrugged. Made sense, he figured, if you were going to use a lot of drop passes and back passes. He'd noticed himself how often the puck rolled off the backside curve of his blade. He just couldn't be as accurate with back passes as he was with forward.

"What make is it?" he asked.

"That's what's really strange," said Sarah. "It looks homemade – almost like somebody carved it out of a tree branch."

6

THERE WAS A GOOD CROWD TO WATCH THE
Rideau Rebels play the Screech Owls. The
Rebels were the media favourite in the tournament. Not only was the team made up of local
kids, it was the namesake of one of the first teams
ever to play in the Ottawa area. The modern
Rebels even wore replica jerseys.

According to the *Citizen* newspaper, if there
hadn't once been a team called the Rebels, there
would never have been a Stanley Cup. Two of the
players on the team had been the sons of Lord
Stanley, the Governor General of the day. Lord
Stanley, who had come over from England, never
tried to play himself, but he enjoyed watching,
and at the end of his appointment in Canada he
decided to leave behind a "challenge cup" for
hockey teams to play for. Lord Stanley spent
$48.67 of his own money on the trophy, but never
once saw it played for. He could not have imagined that, a century after he'd returned home to
England, the Stanley Cup would be the most
easily recognized trophy in professional sport.

Two of the Rebels' players, Kenzie MacNeil and James Grove, were the *Citizen*'s choice as most likely candidates for the Most Valuable Player award, which was to be presented on the final day by the modern Governor General. If the award were to go to one of the two Rebels, said the *Citizen*, it would be "poetic justice."

"What the heck's *that* mean?" Nish demanded when Travis showed him the article.

"That it should happen. That it's the right thing."

"Yeah, *right*!" Nish said with great sarcasm.

Nish didn't miss a beat. Just before the puck dropped on the opening faceoff, he skated past Kenzie MacNeil, lining up to face off against Sarah, and quickly whispered his own version of "poetic justice":

"Roses are red, violets are blue.
I'll be MVP – not you."

MacNeil just looked at him and shook his head, baffled.

Halfway through the shift Travis could see why Kenzie MacNeil might be the early favourite as the tournament's top player. Joe Hall had switched the lineups around a bit, perhaps sensing that Nish and Sam would hardly be able to play together. Nish was out with Lars, and Lars made the mistake of trying to jump into the play right after the faceoff. Sarah tied up MacNeil, but just as Lars tried to slip in and away with the puck, MacNeil used his skate to drag the puck through the circle and up onto his stick. Sarah stuck with him, but he was able, one-handed, to flick a backhand pass to his left winger, James Grove, who suddenly had open ice with Lars out of the picture.

Nish cut fast across the blueline to cover for Lars, but to do so he had to leave the far wing open. The Rebel left winger was able to fire a rink-wide pass, blind, knowing that the Rebels' other winger would be open.

Travis was the Owls' only hope. He chased his check and caught him just inside the Owls' blueline. Travis began leaning on the player to force him off towards the boards, but he should have tried to play the puck. The winger flipped an easy drop pass that looped over Travis's stick and fell, like a spinning plate, on the safe side of the line.

Kenzie MacNeil, moving up fast, was all alone. He came in on Jeremy – who was coming out to cut the angle – and instead of cutting, or faking a shot, MacNeil simply hauled back and slammed a vicious slapshot that tore right through Jeremy's pads and popped out the other side into the Screech Owls net.

As the starting lineup skated off, their heads hung low, Sarah said to Nish,

*"Roses are red, violets are blue,
When that guy scored, where were you?"*

"Ahhh, drop it!" Nish said angrily, slamming his stick down.

Travis felt bad for his friend. He'd seen that Nish had simply tried to cover for Lars, who made the initial mistake, and that in doing so he'd left his side open and gave the Rebels the opening they needed. Sarah was also at fault, Travis said to himself, for she was supposed to have stayed with MacNeil. He'd learned long ago, however, that there was no point in arguing over what had happened out there. The only thing that mattered was what would happen *next* – and the Screech Owls had to get back into this game.

"Everyone noticed how they scored that goal, I hope," said Joe Hall. "Drop pass."

Joe Hall decided to counter the Rebels' big scoring line by putting Sam out every time MacNeil was on the ice. Sam's only job was to stay back and make sure the big Rebel centre didn't get free. As the game continued, she stuck to him, in Nish's words, "like gum to the bottom of a school chair," and it was clear that the star player was growing frustrated.

So, too, was Nish, who was not seeing his usual amount of ice time. On a Rebels power play he let little James Grove slip in behind him, and the talented Rebel got away a hard shot that Jeremy in goal took on the shoulder, sending the puck flipping high over the boards. The whistle put an end to play, but Nish continued right on through the little forward, running him over like a Zamboni and picking up a second penalty for the Owls.

Joe Hall was not amused. He waited until Nish returned to the bench from the penalty box, then very calmly he told him he had all but cost them the game with that stupid after-the-whistle hit.

"If you can't control your temper," Joe Hall said in a steady voice that must have sounded like a scream in Nish's burning ears, "you'll never control the play."

Nish didn't play another shift. Joe Hall began double-shifting Sam, pairing her first with Lars and then Wilson – and the more she played the more she shone.

In the second period, Gordie Griffith picked up a bouncing puck at centre and broke up alone, dishing off to Dmitri, who was just coming over the boards on the fly. Dmitri raced in and beat the Rebels' goaltender with his trademark backhand high into the net.

MacNeil might have scored a second when he got in alone, but a sprawling, stick-swinging desperation move by Sam knocked the puck off his stick and into the corner as she fell to the ice. MacNeil came to a sharp stop, his skates deliberately throwing snow into Sam's face.

She got up, laughing.

If it had been Nish, he would have come up swinging.

In the third, the two teams exchanged goals: one by Fahd on a weak, looping shot from the point that bounced in off the butt of one of the Rebels' defenders – "*Exactly the way I planned it!*" Fahd claimed at the bench – and one by the Rebels when little James Grove came down one-on-one and slipped the puck through Wilson's skates. The little Rebel then pulled out Jeremy just as deftly, sliding the puck in so slowly it looked like he was in a curling match.

Travis had one good chance. He broke up ice with Sarah charging behind him through centre, but when he tried to cut to the defence and drop the puck for Sarah – a no-no, according to Muck – he blew the opportunity, leaving the puck for the second defenceman instead. The defenceman simply chipped the puck off the boards and the Rebels had a three-on-two that, once again, Sam foiled with a poke check.

"You have to get the puck to your centre," Joe Hall said when Travis skated off. "It's not a package you leave at the front desk for her to pick up when she's got time."

Travis nodded, knowing he'd blown it. Next time, if there was a next time, he'd make sure the puck was on Sarah's stick before taking himself out of the play.

But there was no second chance for Travis. The horn blew — a 2–2 tie — and the teams lined up to shake hands. Travis was right behind Sam. Big Kenzie MacNeil was coming through the line, barely touching hands rather than shaking them. When he came to Sam, he scowled.

"Keep off my case," he hissed, "or I'll take you out."

Sam yanked off her helmet and shook out her bright red hair. She blinked several times, faking delight.

"My, my, Kenzie," she said, smiling, "are you asking me out on a *date*?"

It was MacNeil's turn to blink — but in genuine surprise. Had he not realized Sam was a girl?

"*Go to hell!*" he snarled.

He refused to shake Sam's hand, slamming his fist into Travis's glove instead and turning abruptly to leave the line.

Sam was laughing loudly.

It was a good thing, Travis thought, that Joe Hall had already ordered Nish to the dressing room.

Sam had scored another bull's eye, and Nish would not have been pleased.

7

"WHERE ARE MY GAUCHIES?"

The players had just come back from an early-morning dip in the Ottawa River and were supposed to change quickly for the long bus ride to Algonquin Park. Nish had been first in the water, first out of the water, first dried off, and first back to the tent. Travis was only stepping off the beach when he heard the yells from inside their tent.

"WHO TOOK MY GAUCHIES?"

Travis hurried up, pulled back the flaps, and there was Nish, buck naked in the centre of the tent, kicking everyone's sleeping bags and clothes as fast as his feet could move. He seemed near panic.

"My boxers are gone!" he shouted at Travis, as if Travis would know what had become of them. *"All of them. What the hell's going on here?"*

"Calm down," Travis said. "You've just misplaced them like you do with everything."

"Somebody's stolen them."

"Who'd want to touch *your* boxer shorts?" Fahd asked as he ducked inside.

42

"That's what *I* want to know," cried Nish, missing Fahd's point.

Travis, who was the most organized, led them on a careful check of all their clothes. This wasn't the first time they'd been on a hunt like this: Travis still chuckled when he remembered how Nish's boxers had once ended up in the freezer. The boys carefully made piles of Lars's stuff, and Fahd's, and Andy's, Jesse's, Dmitri's, Travis's, Nish's – but nowhere could they find any of Nish's distinctive yellow-and-green boxer shorts.

"Call the police," Nish said.

"And what?" Travis asked. "Ask them to put out an all-points-bulletin on missing underwear? You'll just have to borrow some."

"Not mine!" said Fahd with alarm.

"Not mine!"

"Not mine, either!"

"Nor mine!"

"Forget it," Nish said angrily. "They're all too small anyway."

They poked around in the clothes some more, but it was futile. Finally Nish sighed heavily, a sign that he was giving up.

"What'll you do?" asked Fahd.

"Go naked, pal – that okay with you? Will you mind my big white butt sitting on your lap?"

"Oh, God!" said Fahd. "Can't you find something?"

"You can wear your bathing suit," Travis suggested. "We'll probably be swimming again anyway."

"It's wet."

"So what? Put it on."

Nish made a face and stepped back into his bathing suit, then pulled his wide khaki shorts over top. The wet bathing suit immediately soaked through to the front of his shorts.

"Jeez," said Nish. "Now I look like I wet myself."

"Better that than naked," said Fahd. "C'mon, let's go – we're already five minutes late."

They finished dressing, grabbed their towels, and ran to catch the team bus, which Mr. Dillinger had already pulled up to the front gate of the camp. The rest of the Owls were already aboard, and a great cheer went up when the stragglers came into sight.

Nish, worried about the wet spots on his shorts, wrapped his swimming towel around himself as he ran. He was last to the bus, and had to wait while the others filed by Mr. Dillinger.

Joe Hall was already there. He shook a finger at each late boy, but didn't really seem all that angry. His eyes went wide when he saw Nish wrapped in a damp towel.

"You got anything on under there, big boy?" shouted Sam from well back in the bus.

Nish looked up, his face reddening. "Somebody

stole my boxers. *You* wouldn't know anything about that, would you?"

The whole bus broke into laughter. They'd been waiting for this moment.

"Check the flagpole!" Jenny shouted.

Nish looked from face to face, but saw no allies, no explanation. Finally, he bent down and leaned towards the window, staring up as far as he could see.

There, at the top of the camp flagpole, Nish's boxer shorts flapped in a gentle breeze.

"Who did that?" Nish asked, unnecessarily.

"*We did!*" the girls on the team all said at once.

"We're all just so grateful for *men's* lingerie," Sam said, her voice almost exactly the same as Nish's at the camp supper.

The bus broke up. Red-faced and furious, Nish bolted past Fahd for a seat by the window. He swept the towel from around his waist and threw it over his head to escape his tormentors.

Mr. Dillinger helped poor Nish out. He slammed a CD of Smashing Pumpkins into the bus player and cranked it up loud.

The bus jumped as it pulled out, wheels spinning and screeching slightly as the dirt changed to pavement. Everyone in the bus broke into a cheer.

They were headed for Algonquin Park.

They were off to visit a ghost.

The "ghosts" had been Mr. Dillinger's idea. He'd spent all of June planning this trip. He'd been delighted when the organizers of the Little Stanley Cup had insisted that the tournament be as much about seeing new things as playing new teams, and he'd enthusiastically signed the Owls up for the river rafting and mountain biking and watching the magnificent fireworks on Parliament Hill.

But the ghost idea had been his alone. He'd read an article about all the ghosts the area could lay claim to, and he asked the Owls if they had any interest in trying to see one. It was a crazy idea – just the sort of brilliant, offbeat activity Mr. Dillinger was so good at coming up with – and they'd cheered the suggestion loudly.

He took them down to Sparks Street and had a local historian point out the precise spot where Thomas D'Arcy McGee, one of the Fathers of Confederation, had been shot in the back by James Patrick Whelan as McGee fiddled with his latch key. The historian was wonderful, even dressing up in period costume to tell the story of the assassin, the last person publicly hanged in Canada. "It happened on February 11, 1869," the historian told them. "The people came by the hundreds, from all over, to watch Whelan hang from the gallows just down the street from here. To this day, there are people who claim the ghost of James Patrick Whelan still walks the streets of

Ottawa on dark, misty nights. And there are those who say Thomas D'Arcy McGee sometimes rises to speak in the House of Commons on nights when Parliament isn't in session."

They'd toured Laurier House, where Prime Minister Sir Wilfrid Laurier had once lived. The staff who looked after the house told them of the strange happenings that had occurred there: furniture that had been moved in the night, lights on in the morning that had been turned off when the house was closed the previous day. They went to the William Lyon Mackenzie King estate in the Gatineau Hills and toured the strange grounds where King, who seemed a madman to the Owls, had brought relics of old churches and buildings from as far away as London, England, and erected them in the woods. A tour guide told them how King, even when he was prime minister, held seances to consult his dead dog and mother on how to run the country.

And now, Mr. Dillinger had said, they were off to visit "the greatest Canadian ghost of them all: Tom Thomson."

It was a long bus ride to Algonquin Park. Some of the Owls slept. Fahd played with his Game Boy. Sarah read. Wilson and Sam listened to hip-hop on their portable CD players. But Travis just turned to the window and stared out at the glittering lakes and endless bush.

They were well inside the park when Travis felt the bus suddenly slow and pull off to the side of the road.

"Shhhhhh," Mr. Dillinger said from the front of the bus. "Everyone out, but keep it quiet."

Travis wasn't sure at first what they were getting out for, but when he stepped down into the bright wincing light of the day he realized the bus was not alone. Several vehicles, some wearing canoes on their roofs like caps, had also stopped. And up ahead, a crowd of visitors had gathered, many of them with cameras raised.

"A moose cow and her calf," whispered Mr. Dillinger. "Go gently."

Travis and Nish pushed through to the front of the crowd. They faced a bog, which farther out gave way to water, and here the moose and her calf were standing, shoulder deep, calmly biting down into the water and then slowly chewing as they gazed about like moose tourists who had suddenly come upon a herd of humans.

"Who chews their water?" Nish asked.

"They're *eating*," said Travis. "There are weeds growing just under the water."

"Gross!" Nish said.

But Travis was fascinated by the big animals and, in particular, by their lack of fear. Surely they had noticed the people standing about, the cars and trucks pulling off to the side of the road and stopping in a cloud of dust. But they seemed, if anything, amused by all the attention.

Travis took a few photographs on his disposable camera and then, almost in an instant, the moose were gone, dark shadows slipping into the darker shadows of the deep bush.

"Wow!" said a voice beside Travis.

It was Sam. She was shaking with excitement. "Did you ever see anything so beautiful?"

Travis didn't know if he had. But it was more than the moose. It was the park itself, so green, so wild, the hills so sudden and the rock cuts so deep, the lakes so blue and clean and inviting. They stopped at the Lake of Two Rivers picnic grounds and had lunch and swam – Nish first in because he was already in his bathing suit – and then continued to Canoe Lake, where the ghost of Tom Thomson was supposedly waiting for them.

"This ghost business is a load of garbage," Nish was saying in a seat far behind Travis. Nish's voice was back to normal: a touch too loud, a bit too confident, a little too much bluster. "It's like UFOs," he said. "You got all these people claiming to see one, but how come nobody's ever got a picture of one?"

"There's lots of pictures of UFOs," said Data, who counted himself an expert on anything to do with space.

"They're all fakes," Nish said.

"How do you know the authorities don't just say that so people don't panic?" said Data. "Just imagine for a second if the government came out and announced that aliens from outer space were really flying over New York or Vancouver – or Algonquin Park, for that matter."

"I'll believe it when I see it for myself," said Nish, as if that was an end to the argument.

They pulled off at Canoe Lake. Mr. Dillinger had arranged everything. There was a barge boat waiting for them at the Portage Store, big enough to hold everyone, as well as a couple of park rangers, one to run the outboard and one, an older man who smoked a pipe, to point out the sights.

On the long run up the lake, the older ranger told the Owls the essentials of the Tom Thomson story. Now Canada's most famous painter, he was unknown when he first came to the park just before the First World War. Some of the rangers at the time thought he should be arrested as a madman for setting up a three-legged stand, resting a board on it, and then slapping paint all over the board. "They'd never ever *heard* of an 'artist'!"

Over the next few summers, however, Thomson had become as much a part of the park as the rangers themselves. They taught him how to paddle a canoe, how to fish for lake trout, how to set up a camp, and how to find his way around the intricate highway of park lakes.

"People came in then by train," said the ranger. "Train's long gone, so's the lodge he stayed at when he wasn't camping. The woman he was engaged to marry died a lonely old woman years ago, convinced to the end that Tom's body still lay in a shallow grave at the top of that hill there with the birch trees."

He pointed to the shore, to a splash of white birch on a small hill overlooking the lake. Travis felt a chill run down his back.

As an island came near, the ranger steering the boat killed the outboard. The silence was shocking. The older ranger waited, knowing he had his audience in the palm of his hand.

"Right here," he said, pointing down into the calm black waters off the island, "is where Tom Thomson's body rose to the surface in July of 1917."

"What happened?" asked Fahd, his eyes wide open.

The ranger shrugged and smiled. "No one knows. Eight days earlier he'd set off from that far point over there on a short fishing trip and never returned. They found his canoe, but never his paddle – and paddles float. So do bodies after a few days in warm water, but they didn't find him for more than a week, and when they did they also found a length of wire wrapped round and round his ankle – almost as if he'd been tied down to something – and a small, bleeding hole in his temple."

"Murder!" Fahd practically shouted.

"Maybe. There'd been a fight the night before, people say, and the lodge owner, Shannon Fraser, had supposedly struck Tom a blow, and Tom fell down and cracked his head on the fire grate. Some say Fraser and his wife dumped Tom overboard that night with something heavy tied to his ankle, and then cast his canoe adrift, hoping people would presume he'd drowned and wasn't ever coming up. Tom had also argued with an American cottager down the way" – he pointed to the opposite shore – "about the war (Canada was in it, the United States not yet) and the story goes that the hole in Tom's temple came from a .22 fired by the cottager as Tom paddled by. There's also those who say he struck his head when he fell in his canoe while standing up to take a leak –"

"*What?*" Nish screeched.

"That's one theory," the ranger said, smiling. "But none of us here put much stock in it. It only takes a few paddle-strokes to reach shore around here – so why would anybody be so stupid?"

"What do *you* think happened?" asked Sarah.

The ranger nodded. "I think he was murdered. I think that's why people say they keep seeing him come back. He's trying to tell us something."

8

THEY TIED THE BOAT UP TO A SMALL ISLAND —
Little Wapomeo, the old ranger called it — and
explored before taking another swim. The Screech
Owls were getting hungry again, and the rangers
were already making a fire as the players dried off
and strung their towels over a rope the younger
ranger had strung between two spruce trees. There
were hot dogs and marshmallows to toast, and cold
canned pop. Mr. Dillinger had certainly planned
well. And long after they'd eaten their fill they
continued to sit around the fire, talking easily with
the rangers about their fascinating jobs.

Travis noticed that it was quickly getting dark.
The smoke from the fire was gathering about the
island. There was also a mist rising from the water,
swirling and shifting mysteriously as if something
unseen were controlling the air currents.

He watched the older ranger and Joe Hall for
a while, the two of them standing down by the
water and talking quietly. Travis couldn't hear
what they were saying.

When the ranger came back he had his pipe
out and was poking at it with his jackknife. He

loaded it up again and made a great show of lighting the pipe from a flaming stick he plucked from the fire. He sat down on a large block of wood, leaned forward, and began what everyone had been waiting for – the tale of Tom Thomson's ghost.

Travis couldn't stop shivering. It was partly that the day was cooling down, partly the way the smoke from the fire and the mist from the lake moved about the edge of the island like dancing clouds, and partly the tone of the older ranger's voice as he told the story.

Tom Thomson's body had surfaced, "all swollen and coming apart, white skin waving in the water," and his fiancée, Miss Trainor from the cottage across the way (he pointed with his pipe), had demanded to see the body. No one wanted her to see it, but she insisted. She would believe to her dying day that this had been no accident.

"They buried him right away. Had to. Not to put too fine a point on it, he was rotting. They took him by cart up that hill I showed you, wrapped him in a cloth, and buried him. Next day this undertaker shows up, claims he's been sent by the Thomson family, and refuses any offers of help to dig up the body so he can take it back to where the family lived.

"The undertaker went up there with a big black coffin and a lantern and worked through the dark night. In the morning, when the men went up by horse and cart to get him, he was sitting there happy as a clam, the coffin all sealed up and ready to go.

"Some of the men – and I knew some of them, too – claimed he hadn't done a thing. Couldn't have done anything; nobody could dig up and move that body all by himself. One of the rangers who helped load the coffin on the train said he could hear sand sliding inside. The sand all slid to one side when they set it down. Shouldn't have done that if a body was inside, should it?"

"No," answered Fahd unnecessarily.

"There was a lot never explained about this. If they took his body, how come his fiancée, Miss Trainor, kept cleaning up his grave there on that hill? She did it for more'n forty years – right up until she died.

"A few years back a bunch of men on the lake decided to check and dug up where Tom'd been buried. Found a skeleton there with a hole in the skull. Government and police came in and investigated and claimed it wasn't Tom at all but some Indian. Said he'd probably been buried there long, long ago. Makes no sense to me. No Indians around here that I ever knew of – but they always said Tom Thomson looked like he was Indian with those high cheekbones of his.

"One of the old-timers on the lake even said there was a third grave, that they'd gone up and stolen Tom's body away after the first burial up on the hill to make sure he stayed here at Canoe Lake — and that was why the undertaker had nothing but sand in his coffin. He wouldn't admit he couldn't find anything, see?"

"Yeah," said Fahd,

"This old guy said he was going to show people once and for all what had happened. Told his story one late winter's day to a newspaper reporter, and then came back here to that old house up the narrows where he and his brother lived. Was walking across the iced-over lake with their groceries when he fell through — right there, believe it, right at the spot where they found Tom."

No one said a word this time. A loon called far out on the lake, sending shivers up more than a dozen spines. The fire cracked, causing several of the Owls to jump.

"There was a woman, lived here for years, and she swore that on a night with a mist just like this she got lost in her canoe. This man in a canoe slips out of the mist, smiles, and guides her back to shore. She swore it was Tom — but he'd been dead nearly twenty years.

"Another time two guides were travelling behind a party of American fishermen when a man suddenly appeared out of the mist and called towards them that there'd been a drowning at the rapids up ahead. Sure enough, when they got there one of the American fishermen's canoes had gone over and a man was lost. Both guides swore it had been Tom who called to them.

"There's some say you can hear him paddling by on a night like this . . ."

The ranger cocked his ear. The silence was astonishing, and all strained to listen. The loon called again. The fire sparked. Travis could hear the light lick of water – Tom paddling? – but realized after a while it was just the lake playing on the rocks along the shore.

They sat a moment, the smoke and mist swirling about them.

"*I think I hear him now!*" the ranger said in an urgent whisper.

They strained to hear.

"*What a crock!*" Nish whispered in Travis's ear.

"*Look to the point!*" the ranger hissed.

Travis looked, but could see nothing. He strained and thought he could sense the mist moving, and a distant object growing. It had to be his imagination.

But it wasn't. The object, whatever it was, grew closer, and slowly the sound of a canoe in the water fell over the camp and drowned out all other sound, their ears filling with the light kiss of a well-stroked paddle on water. It was almost as if a wind had come up – suddenly the mist parted and a dark canoe slid out of the night, the water licking on the sides, the bow sizzling lightly as it broke the water.

"OH MY GOD!" screamed Sam, bringing everyone to their feet.

"*Fake!*" whispered Nish. "*What a wuss she is!*"

The canoe came closer. The older ranger
moved back, as if caught by surprise, and as he
moved, everyone moved.

"*Who goes there?*" he called. There was real
urgency in his voice.

Sam screamed. Nish giggled.

But Sam wasn't the only one frightened.
Travis could hear Fahd whimper. There was a
quick shuffling movement on the shore now,
almost as if all the Owls were trying to gather so
tight together they would become one.

The canoe came closer, closer.

At that moment a white light appeared on the
water. Cast up from inside the canoe, it revealed
a man paddling. His face, streaked with dark
shadow, was ferocious.

Sam screamed!

Jenny screamed!

Lars screamed!

Jesse screamed!

Sam screamed again!

Travis remembered his disposable camera. It
was in his pocket. He pulled it out.

The flash exploded like sunlight over the
scene. For an instant, they could see everything:
the grey-green canoe, the dark-haired paddler,
his paddle raised for the next stroke . . .

Then the flash was gone. And at the same instant the light casting shadows on the paddler's face was gone, and, in another instant, the canoe itself was gone, with not even the sound of a paddle touching water.

"*What the devil was that?*" the ranger asked.

"T–Tom T–Thomson," Fahd suggested.

"*Wow!*" whispered Nish with great sarcasm. "*How'd he ever figure that out?*"

"I don't . . . know," the ranger said. "I've never seen anything like that before in my life." He sounded shaken.

"*He probably sees it every week at exactly the same time,*" hissed Nish.

Travis didn't know what to think. If it had been a trick, it was a spectacularly successful one. He was shaking like a leaf, and so, too, he suspected, were the others. Probably even Nish.

But it couldn't have been a real ghost. It couldn't have been Tom Thomson – could it? No. Not possible.

"Check around," whispered Nish. "Where's Joe Hall?"

Travis looked about the campsite. He could account for everyone – the two rangers, Mr. Dillinger, the Screech Owls – but not Joe Hall. Nish might have guessed correctly. Had Joe Hall sneaked off and slipped a canoe into the water on the other side of the island?

But there was Joe Hall now! He was moving near the trees with Sarah and Sam, an arm around each of them. Sam seemed terrified. She was sobbing as she held on to Joe Hall's powerful arm.

"*Look at her!*" hissed Nish. "*She's bawling like a baby. What a wuss!*"

The rangers were already packing up quickly to go. They drowned the fire and loaded the barge and told everyone to get on. Joe Hall held a flashlight so no one would fall climbing on.

A large flashlight? *Perhaps he had also held it between his knees and shone it up onto his face!*

Travis borrowed one of the rangers' flashes on the pretence of helping others pick their way along the shore, and he used it to sweep over Joe Hall and examine him. His knees were soaking wet – *as if he'd been kneeling in a canoe!*

"It was him," announced Nish, delighted with their detective work.

Maybe that was what Joe Hall had been whispering about with the ranger, thought Travis: a plan to trick the Owls into thinking the ghost of Tom Thomson had appeared.

"We'll find out for sure tomorrow," said Travis.

"How's that? You expect him to confess?"

Travis smiled and held out his camera. "I took his picture, remember?"

"I can hardly wait to show her."

"*Her?*" Travis asked.

"*Sam! Who else?*"

9

THE RIDEAU REBELS HAD EASILY WON THEIR next game against the highly touted Vancouver Mountain. The Mountain had, with the Rebels, been the early favourite of the Ottawa press, which meant that now all eyes were on the Screech Owls, who had unexpectedly managed to tie the powerful Rebels in game one. There were other teams in the tournament – including the New Jersey Li'l Devils – but none of the others was expected to challenge for the Little Stanley Cup.

Nish was in a wonderful mood. He'd come back to the camp to find his boxers down from the flagpole and returned to the tent. Even better, he figured he was about to go one-up on Sam, once Travis turned his camera in to the little shop down the road and got his photos back. He'd be delighted to show her what had terrified her at Canoe Lake: the very person she'd run to for comfort.

They arrived at the Kanata Recreation Centre early, and Joe Hall asked Travis if he could see him a moment out in the corridor. *Had he noticed the camera?* Travis wondered. *Was he going to try to get it from him so the identity of "Tom Thomson" would remain a mystery?*

But Joe Hall had no intention of talking about photographs. He had his stick with him – the strange stick that Sarah had noticed was as straight as a ruler and seemed somehow homemade. He told Travis to bring his stick along as well.

With Joe Hall leading the way, the two walked through to the smaller of the two rinks, which was not being used. It was cold and empty, with fog gathering in one corner of the ice surface on such a hot day. It made Travis think momentarily of the canoe in the mist, but Joe Hall didn't want to talk about ghosts either, real or otherwise.

"I like what I see in you, Travis," Joe Hall said.

"Thanks," said Travis.

Joe Hall dropped a puck he had been carrying in his pocket. It sounded like a rifle shot in the empty rink. He stickhandled back and forth a few times, the straight blade as comfortable on one side of the puck as the other.

"You had a chance to win that opener for us, you know," Joe Hall said.

"I guess," admitted Travis. He knew what the coach was getting at. The drop pass to Sarah that didn't work.

"I want you to stand on the blueline," said Joe Hall. "And just watch something – okay?"

"Okay," said Travis.

Travis hurried to the blueline, sliding easily in his sneakers. He wished he was in his skates. He'd feel taller, more himself.

Joe Hall began moving away from Travis towards the net, stickhandling easily. He moved almost as if daydreaming, the puck clicking regularly from one side to the other as he moved in and stared, as if a goalie were there, waiting.

Suddenly there was a louder click – and the puck was shooting straight back at Travis! It was right on Travis's blade, but it had happened so fast it caught him completely off guard. Travis fumbled the pass, letting the puck jump outside the blueline.

"How'd you do that?" Travis asked.

"Fire it back," said Joe Hall. "And this time be ready for it."

Travis passed the puck back. Joe Hall again stickhandled back and forth, the steady click of puck on wood almost soothing. Then the louder click – and the puck was shooting back at Travis! He was ready this time, and could have fired a shot instantly.

"I still don't know how you're doing that!" Travis called.

"Come and see," Joe Hall called back.

Travis skidded on his sneakers to where Joe Hall was waiting. Travis gave him the puck and he stickhandled a bit, then he brought the heel of his stick down hard and fast on the front edge of the puck, sending it like a bullet between his legs and against the corner boards.

Joe Hall looked up and flashed his amazing smile. " 'Rat' Westwick came up with it," he said. "He called it the 'heel pass.' He and 'One-Eyed' Frank McGee used to bamboozle other teams with it. They never knew when it was coming. Watch."

Joe Hall retrieved the puck and stickhandled again, effortlessly, and then suddenly the heel came down hard on the puck instead of passing over it again, and the puck shot, true and accurately, right between Joe Hall's legs and into the corner.

"Let me try," said Travis.

He took the puck, stickhandled, and chopped down, but the puck stayed where it was.

"You have to hit the front edge," said Joe Hall.

Travis tried again. This time the puck flew, but into his own feet. It wasn't clean and straight like it was when Joe Hall did it.

"It's your stick," said Joe Hall. "Try mine."

Travis handed over his new stick – Easton, special curve, narrow shaft, ultralight – and took Joe Hall's from him.

It felt heavy. It felt wrong. He set the blade on the ice, and it looked to the left-handed Travis like a right-hand stick. As if the curve was going the wrong way. But it wasn't a right stick either; it was perfectly straight. There was no name on it, only "J. Hall" pencilled near the top of the handle.

"Where'd you buy this thing?" Travis said.

"You can't buy them," said Joe Hall. He didn't offer where it had come from.

Travis worked the puck back and forth. He lost it several times, being used to the cup of a curve that was no longer there.

"Try the heel pass," Joe Hall said.

Travis did. The stick came down perfectly on the puck, and it shot straight and true between his legs. Joe Hall was waiting and timed a shot perfectly with Travis's stick. The puck stuck high in the far corner of the net.

"Wow!" said Travis. "That worked perfectly."

"You like to try the stick in a game?" Joe Hall asked.

Travis felt the stick again. It still didn't feel right to him. "Maybe," he said, looking up to make sure he wasn't hurting Joe Hall's feelings. "But I'm so used to mine."

Joe Hall took his stick back and handed Travis his. "Suit yourself," he said. "But you'll never master the heel pass with that curved blade."

Game two was against the Sudbury Minors, a gritty little team with tremendous heart but limited talent. The Owls jumped to a quick three-goal lead on a clean breakaway by Dmitri, a hard blast by Andy, and an exquisite end-to-end rush by Sarah in which she split the Sudbury defence and roofed a backhand as she fell into the corner.

Travis noticed almost immediately when Nish began to wander. Had Muck been here, he would have called Nish on it immediately, but Joe Hall was new to the team, and Mr. Dillinger and Data had other duties apart from trying to figure out when Nish was about to go off the deep end.

The first hint was on a play when icing was waved off and Nish picked up the puck in his own corner and failed to hit Sarah with the usual breakout pass. Instead, Nish started his old river-hockey routine, trying to stickhandle through the entire team so he could be the hero and score the goal. He made it all the way down the ice, moving superbly, but he cranked his shot off the crossbar. Which only made matters worse from then on. Now Nish was absolutely determined to score.

Travis could see Joe Hall's frustration mounting. He told Nish to stay back, but Nish ignored him. The Owls were up 6–0 when Nish tried a stupid play. Turning his stick backwards, he tried to skate up the ice with the puck held by the knob of the handle.

Muck hated hot-dogging. Perhaps it was because Muck wasn't here that Nish was getting so out of control, but he picked the wrong team to try to humiliate. The Sudbury team might have been a bit low on talent, but they lacked nothing in courage. Nish was barely over centre when the captain of the Minors hit him so hard he flew in a complete somersault. He landed on his skates, wobbling a bit before he crashed into the boards.

The referee was signalling charging. Nish should have been happy – it would have given the Owls the advantage – but he wanted revenge. He jumped to his feet and charged the Sudbury captain back. The crowd roared as Nish put his shoulder into his opponent. The big Minors captain never moved. Nish shook off his gloves, deliberately tossing them so they struck the other player. The linesmen moved in quickly before anything could happen. Nish was lucky the referee called him only for roughing – one blow would have meant an automatic game ejection.

Nish knew his shifts were over when he finally got out of the penalty box. He skated casually across the ice to the Screech Owls' bench and yanked open the gate.

"Wrong door," said Joe Hall, his lips tight.

"What do you mean?" asked Nish.

"The Zamboni doors for you, buddy. You're through this game, *and the next*. We don't need that."

Nish's mouth went so round it could have held a puck.

"W–w–what?" he stammered.

"You heard me. Get off the ice."

Nish looked desperately around for support, but he found none, and then began to make his way to the far end of the rink. He stared at his teammates as he passed by, but none would look back. None except Sam.

She laughed.

Nish paused, about to say something stupid, but then thought better of it. He didn't need any more trouble from Joe Hall.

The game seemed to die after that. Sudbury had clearly given up, and thanks to lessons taught them by Muck Munro, the Owls weren't inclined to run up the score any further.

They played the clock out cleanly and quickly, working more on their passing than their shots, careful at all times to remain in position.

Travis had one glorious moment near the end of the game when Dmitri flipped a pass high from his own blueline and Travis gloved it down right at the red line. He had the puck, and he had space to work. He looked up: one defence back, Sarah coming up clear from her own end.

Travis began moving with the puck, happy with the way it felt on his stick, glad he'd stuck to the Easton instead of taking up Joe Hall's offer of the straight blade.

He cut towards centre, the defence keeping an eye on him but refusing to commit. Travis worked the puck across the blueline, then cut across again so that he drew the defender with him while Sarah moved across the blueline and into position.

He laid the puck out in front, exactly where he wanted it. He stickhandled once, twice, then came down hard on the puck with the heel of the stick.

The puck shot to the side and into the corner!

The play had failed, but it had still fooled the defence, who turned to chase the lost puck. Sarah was there ahead of him, and she quickly fired the puck back to Travis, who snapped it into the open side.

Screech Owls 7, Sudbury Minors 0.

He had scored, and his teammates were cheering, but Travis knew he had failed. He looked up at Joe Hall as he came off the ice, teammates slapping his pants and shoulders.

"Wrong stick," said Joe Hall.

"I know," said Travis.

"It's there any time you want it."

Travis smiled, not yet ready. "Thanks," he said. "Maybe next game."

10

"I'VE FIGURED IT OUT," NISH SAID.

Travis didn't dare ask what. *How to behave during a hockey game? How to be a real team player? How Joe Hall pulled off that Tom Thomson stunt?* It could have been anything.

They were lying in the tent, a light rain drumming on the canvas. They'd practised earlier and had eaten and were resting.

"Figured what out?" Fahd finally asked. He couldn't resist.

"How I'm going to get her."

"Get who?"

"Oh, just the one who tried to make a fool of me on the river, just the one who put my gauchies up the flagpole, just the biggest pain in the butt this team has ever known, that's all."

Travis couldn't resist. "Who's that?" he asked.

"Very funny," said Nish. He was sucking loudly on a Tootsie Roll, offering none around as usual, and thinking out loud, also as usual. "It's got to be embarrassing, right? Really embarrassing."

"Why?" Fahd asked.

"Because she embarrassed me. All that 'Ka-wa-bun-ga' crap and stealing my boxers. It's got to be just as good from my side."

"Let it go," said Travis. "She's a good sport. The team likes her."

"This isn't about the team," countered Nish. "This is about her and me."

"You're too competitive," said Lars.

"Not at all," said Nish. "I'm just getting even. Like in a tie game. What's competitive about that? I don't have to win, just get even."

Yeah, right, Travis thought to himself. *Who's he kidding?* But he said nothing.

Nish went on. "You know where the women's washroom is?"

"You mean the outhouse," Fahd corrected.

"Whatever – you know where I mean."

"You'd better be careful there," warned Travis.

"Nah. She has to go sometime, doesn't she? I mean, girls do go to the bathroom, don't they?"

Lars couldn't believe it. "You want us to sing, '*We-know-where-you're-go-ing!*'? That's a bit childish even for *you*, isn't it?"

"Nah, no singing. I got a much more sophisticated plan than that. Say she goes in and shuts the door, and a few seconds later there's this enormous explosion that everybody in the camp hears. You think she wouldn't find that a bit embarrassing?"

"You can't bomb an outhouse!" protested Fahd.

"Not a bomb, stupid – a harmless cannon cracker. Like the ones they set off on Canada Day."

"Where are you going to get a cannon cracker?"

"They sell fireworks at that little shop," he said.

"Not to kids they don't," said Travis.

"They'll sell to me," said Nish. "Just you watch."

"How would that work?" Fahd asked. "How would you set it off, even if you got some fireworks?"

"Very simple. The boys' outhouse is right next to it. I run a fuse from one to the other and you signal me."

"*Who?*" they all asked at once.

"*You!*" Nish said loudly. "*My friends, that's who?*"

"Those pictures should be ready," Travis said later that afternoon. "You want to come pick them up with me?"

"I'll be right there," Nish said. First, however, he dashed into the tent. Travis thought he was writing something down. It wasn't like Nish to keep a diary.

"What was that all about?" Travis asked when Nish returned. "Writing home?"

"You'll see," Nish answered. "Let's get going."

It was a brief walk down the highway to the store. It had everything – food, milk, videos to rent, live bait, a film drop-off and, of course, fireworks. It was run by an elderly couple. The woman was French – Sarah had talked with her for quite a while – and her husband was hard of hearing. Apart from Sarah, no one was able to have much of a conversation with either of them.

"I'm here to pick up my pictures," Travis said as they entered the store.

"Eh?" the old man called back, cupping a hand behind his ear.

"My photos," Travis said, louder. "They're supposed to be ready today." He waved his pick-up slip. The old man recognized it and grabbed it out of Travis's hand. He led him to the rear of the store, where the film was kept.

Nish wandered over to the old woman. He smiled his best Nish smile, the smile that meant something unexpected was coming.

Travis couldn't see what was going on. The old man was rummaging through the photos waiting to be picked up, checking Travis's slip against a dozen numbers. Nish and the old woman were bent over a sheet of paper, the old woman asking questions.

Finally the old man came up with the processed film. He handed it over to Travis. "That'll be $12.81, young man."

Travis fumbled with his wallet. Just like Nish, he thought, to make himself scarce when the bills were being paid. He knew Nish would be first to scoop up the picture that showed Joe Hall in the Tom Thomson canoe.

Travis paid up and left. Nish was standing at the front door, counting out his own change. He had a large bag under his arm.

"What's in there?" Travis asked.

"I'll tell you outside. You get the pictures?"

"Yeah, let's go."

Once out and back on the highway, Nish looked around like a man about to hold up a bank. Then he pulled open the bag so Travis could look in.

Inside were dozens of firecrackers: some large, some small and attached to lengths of string, even a few rockets and Roman candles.

"How did you get all that?"

"I bought 'em. She even threw in a few extra for free."

"You can't buy fireworks. You're not old enough."

Nish grinned. "Apparently I am – when I have a note from the church camp that this is for a special ceremony."

"*You lied?*" Travis asked, exasperated with his friend.

Nish shrugged innocently, looking deeply offended.

"Lie? Me? Where's the lie? The note was written on church camp stationery. And it is going to be a special ceremony – a *very* special ceremony."

"But you wrote the note yourself!"

"We never discussed that," Nish said triumphantly. "She didn't ask, so I didn't say."

"And you can't call your stupid plan a 'special ceremony.'"

"It will be when you see it, pal. It will be, I promise you. Now let's have a look at those pictures."

Reluctantly, Travis peeled open the flap of the envelope. He pulled the photos out and began thumbing through them. The moose. The picnic grounds. The barge. . . . He could see the edge of the next photo, showing mist and water.

Travis held his breath. Now they would know. He pulled the photograph free of the others.

It was Canoe Lake all right, the mist swirling on the water. *But nothing else!*

"*You blew it!*" Nish said angrily.

"But I couldn't have. I caught him perfectly."

"You blew it, obviously. There's nothing there. You either snapped too soon or too late.

You blew it – and now I got nothing to shove under Sam's nose."

Nish yanked the photo away and spun it into the ditch. He patted his haul of fireworks. "Thank heaven I got this. Good thing *somebody's* reliable," he said, and began walking back to the camp.

Travis made his way down into the ditch and retrieved the photograph from where it had lodged in a milkweed plant. He started walking, well behind Nish, who was hurrying ahead, happily swinging his bag full of treasure. He carefully studied the photo again.

Nothing.

Nish was right. He'd failed to catch the canoe or the person paddling in it. Too soon or too late.

But it made no sense. How could it show nothing? Travis wondered.

He'd seen the canoe light up when the flash went off – how else would they have known that the canoe had been grey-green, the same colour as Tom Thomson's canoe? And yet this photograph showed nothing but mist and water.

No canoe.

No paddler.

Could it really have been Tom Thomson's ghost? No, Travis decided. Impossible.

But if it was Joe Hall pulling a trick – he remembered the flashlight and the wet knees – then where was Joe Hall? Why was *he* not in the picture?

11

"THIS GAME IS A MUST WIN FOR US," SAID JOE Hall. He was standing at the front of the dressing room, leaning on his straight-as-a-ruler stick. He seemed worried.

More than worried, thought Travis. He looked ill. His face was pasty, and he was sweating. And it seemed, at times, as if he was leaning on the stick for support.

Nish remained in the corner, arms folded. He was the only Screech Owl not dressed. He sat by his locker, staring defiantly. *If this game is so darned important*, he seemed to be saying, *how come I'm not playing?*

"I know what you're thinking," said Joe Hall, almost as if Nish had been talking out loud. He walked over to Nish and prodded him gently with his stick. He smiled, but the smile had lost its former brilliance.

"Joe doesn't look very good," Sarah whispered beside Travis. She had noticed as well.

"You might make a difference in the game," Joe Hall said to Nish. "You might make *the* difference."

Nish seemed happy to hear this. Travis could tell his best friend was fighting off a big smile.

"I'm not a fool," Joe Hall continued. "I can tell when a player has talent or not – and you, sir, have big talent. You might well make the difference in the game . . ." He paused, seeming to have to gather his energy. " But this game can make a difference in your life . . . and I think that's more important."

Nish looked up. He didn't have a clue what Joe Hall was getting at.

"You've got a temper, haven't you?" he said to Nish.

Nish shrugged.

Joe Hall turned to the team. "He's got a temper, doesn't he?"

"The worst," said Sarah.

Nish sneered at her.

"I had a temper," Joe Hall said. "It was the worst part of my game. It almost cost me my career. I had to learn to control it, or else. Who was it asked me what my nickname was the other day?"

"I did," said Fahd, raising his hand like he had to go to the bathroom.

"Well, I didn't tell you what it was, did I?"

"No," said Fahd, his hand still up.

"They called me 'Bad' Joe Hall – and I hated it."

No one spoke. They could hear the sound of Mr. Dillinger's skate-sharpening machine hard at work in the corridor. Joe Hall stumbled slightly, caught himself on Nish's locker. Nish looked up, frightened, but whether he thought Joe Hall was going to fall on him or strike him, Travis couldn't tell.

"You're too good a kid to get hit with a tag like that," said Joe Hall. "Besides, 'Bad' Wayne Nishikawa sounds pretty stupid, doesn't it?" He smiled, and for an instant the old brilliance was back.

Nish was flushing red. "I don't know," he mumbled. Travis knew what Nish was thinking: he'd *love* a nickname like that!

"You play *with* a label, you *become* that label," said Joe Hall. "People came to see 'Bad' Joe Hall, so I gave them 'Bad' Joe Hall – and by the time I realized how stupid I was being . . . it was too late."

Travis knew that Joe Hall was talking about Nish, and about how Nish had to grow up if he ever wanted to be a real player. But there was something more he was trying to say, something about Joe Hall himself. And Travis didn't know what.

"So you're going to watch this game," said Joe Hall. "And I want you to watch a particular player out there all game long – and learn from her. Understand?"

Nish looked up, eyes batting in confusion. "*Her?*" he asked.

"Sam."

"*Sam?*" Nish asked, incredulous.

"Yes, Sam. She's so good at letting nothing get under her skin, she ends up under *their* skin. You saw it the other games."

Joe Hall was right. Sam laughed when she was dumped. She laughed when Kenzie MacNeil sprayed snow in her face. She just laughed, then she kept on doing whatever would drive them crazy.

"I have to watch her?" Nish asked, not believing.

"Every single shift," said Joe Hall. "Now let's get out there!"

The Screech Owls rose to cheers and back-slapping. Travis, as team captain, waited to go out last, and he alone saw the exchange of glances between Nish and Sam as she left the dressing room.

Sam's eyes filled with triumph.

Nish's eyes squeezed tight with revenge.

Sam was certainly well worth watching against the Vancouver Mountain. The Owls were in tough, with the Mountain also having a real chance of reaching the final if only they could beat the Screech Owls. The Rideau Rebels had easily won their third game against the team from

New Jersey, and were sitting atop the standings, waiting only to discover who they would meet in the final: the Owls or the Mountain.

The Mountain were looking to win. They were quick, smart, and strong. By the end of the first, with Jenny struggling in the Screech Owls' net, the Mountain were ahead 3–0. If they could hang on to their lead, they were on their way to the final.

Travis had several chances, but couldn't seem to get a good shot. As soon as he took possession of the puck in the Mountain end, they closed in on him and took away any space for him to work with. He tried setting up Sarah and Dmitri, but the Mountain were keying on Sarah's playmaking and Dmitri's speed and neither of them ever seemed free.

Sam began the turnaround midway through the second. She had already played extremely well, and had yet to be scored on when on the ice, but it was her offensive move that caught the attention of the large crowd. She blocked a shot just inside her own blueline and, still down, used her wide sweep to chip the puck up along the boards by centre. Derek Dillinger beat the Mountain defence to it, sending a cross-ice pass to little Simon Milliken, and Simon crossed the blueline and fired the puck hard around the boards.

Derek made the blueline just in time to keep the puck from sailing out. He kicked it up to his stick, deked towards the boards, then sent a sharp backwards pass to the high slot, where Sam was charging under full steam.

Travis had seen this play before – only it was always Nish charging up centre to join the play late.

Sam faked a slapshot, stepped around the single defence between her and the goal, fired a hard shot the Mountain goalie stopped by stacking his pads, and then clipped her own rebound over him and in under the crossbar.

The tide had turned for the Owls. Inspired by Sam's goal, they kept coming against the strong Mountain team, and soon it seemed only a matter of time until the Owls scored again.

It was Fahd, of all people, who gave them their next goal. He scored his second goal of the tournament on a hard, low shot that screamed right along the ice, through a crowd in front of the net, and caught the goalie by surprise as it ripped just under his stick.

Ten minutes into the third, Sarah took a beautiful pass from Sam and flew up the ice with Dmitri and one defence back. Travis had seen this play a hundred times. Across to Dmitri, back to Sarah; back to Dmitri, the water bottle flying against the glass.

Screech Owls 3, Vancouver Mountain 3.

At the end of regulation they were tied.

The first game had been left with the score

even, but now they needed a tie-breaker to decide which team would advance to the final. The tournament rules called for immediate sudden-death overtime, with four-a-side for the first two minutes, then three-a-side, then two-a-side.

After four minutes with no score, the referee signalled for two-a-side. Travis was halfway over the boards when he felt his sweater being pulled back.

It was Joe Hall. Travis wasn't going.

"Sarah and Sam!" Joe Hall called out.

Travis slunk back onto the bench. He'd been caught by surprise. He'd assumed it would be him and Sarah out – captain and top player – but now it was Sarah and Sam. Two girls. He could see the Rideau Rebels up in the stands, laughing and pointing. The big centre, MacNeil, was on his feet, shouting something, but Travis couldn't make out what it was. He guessed it wasn't complimentary.

He turned and looked at Nish, standing behind the bench in his street clothes. Nish had a smirk on his face and was shaking his head in disbelief.

Things soon changed, however, as Sam chased down a loose puck and used her powerful body to ride off the Mountain player who got there first. She turned as soon as the puck came free and lifted the puck so high it very nearly hit the clock, the rolling puck falling with a slap just across centre.

Sarah had read the play perfectly. She picked up the puck in full flight, completely free of the defence.

Across the ice, the Mountain coach almost came over the boards screaming. *"Offside! Offside!"* But the linesman had waved it off.

The crowd was on its feet.

Sarah came in gracefully, stickhandling carefully, and moved to her backhand – or so it seemed! She made the motion, but just as it appeared she was shifting to go to the short side, she moved the puck back to her forehand and fired a hard wrist shot.

The Mountain goalie, who had a great glove hand, got a small piece of the shot – but not enough.

The red light came on!

The Mountain coach was screaming again!

The Owls poured over the boards, heading to pile onto Sam and Sarah.

They were going to the final!

Travis threw down his stick and gloves and hurled himself into the writhing mess in the corner. Buried somewhere underneath was the player who had set up the winner and the player who had scored it. He could see neither of them.

But he could see Nish. Still standing on the bench. On his face, a look of shock.

12

"PERFECT! ABSOLUTELY PERFECT!"

Nish sat in the centre of the tent rubbing his hands together and chuckling. Travis had rarely, if ever, seen his friend so pleased with himself.

"I've really outdone myself on this one, I think."

"You've come undone," corrected Travis. "You're nuts."

"It's going to work. I promise you."

Nish had been working away like a mad scientist any chance he got. He'd taken apart several of the larger fireworks, saved all the powder inside, and used the fuses to build one very long one. He'd sneaked into the women's outhouse and wired several cannon crackers deep below the seat. Then he'd run his long fuse out through a crack in the outhouse wall and over to the men's' outhouse a short distance away, where he'd hidden it carefully from sight.

"How did you stand it?" Fahd wanted to know when he heard.

"I held my breath, stupid — and worked in shifts."

"I'd have gagged," said Fahd.

"How are you going to catch her going?" Lars asked.

"She'll have to go sometime," Nish said, lightly clapping his hands together, "and when she does, I'll be there with my trusty lighter."

He pulled out a lighter and flicked it on, holding the flame out for all to see.

"Where'd you get that?" Travis asked.

"My good friends up the road," Nish said.

Travis shook his head. "I don't want to know."

Travis left the mad scientist and his admiring throng and set out to walk around the camp. It was a beautiful afternoon, the day before the final game, and the sun was gold and dancing on the river. There was a pair of Canada geese near the shore with a family of puffy little ones, and Travis watched awhile and tried to take his mind off everything. Nish's mad scheme. The mysterious photograph. Joe Hall.

He was worried about Joe Hall. Sarah had noticed the coach's ill health as well, but he'd seemed to rally for the game against the Vancouver Mountain, and by game's end they'd forgotten all about it.

Travis decided to track down Joe Hall and see for himself how he was doing. He headed up the nature trail that led out past the point. His cottage had to be somewhere up that direction.

"Hey! Where're ya goin'?"

It was Sarah. He turned and waved back.

"Just going for a walk."

Sarah smiled. "Like some company?"

"Sure."

Sarah hurried to join him on the trail. "You're looking for Joe Hall, aren't you?" she said in a quiet voice.

"I guess," Travis answered. He really wasn't sure what he was trying to do.

They walked out past the point, then took to the shoreline and made their way upstream. The bush was tangled and the rocks sharp, but by working half through knee-deep water and half through the underbrush, they steadily made their way.

There was no sign of a cottage.

"*Hey!*" a voice called. "*What're you kids up to?*"

Travis and Sarah stopped dead in their tracks. They tried to make out who it was through the thick brush, but could only see a figure moving and a flash of something yellow. Yellow fur.

It was a dog – the setter that belonged to the farmer who cut the grass at the camp. Travis felt his heart begin to beat again.

"Hi!" Sarah called when the farmer came into sight. The setter raced at them, leaping high in an attempt to lick Sarah. She caught the dog by the fur of its collar, settling it and patting it gently.

The farmer seemed to recognize them now. "Youse two are from the camp, eh?"

"Yeah. I'm Travis Lindsay. This is Sarah Cuthbertson."

"You both swim?"

"Yes."

"Well, you got to be careful walking along there, you know. Not much of a current here, but enough to drown more than a few that slipped in."

"We'll be careful," said Travis. "We're looking for Joe Hall's cottage."

"Who?"

"Joe Hall – our coach for the tournament. He's staying in a cottage up here."

The farmer shook his head. He took off his cap, sweat heavy on his brow, and rubbed it off with his shirt sleeve.

"No Hall along here," he said. "No cottage for that matter. Next property north is a park."

"There's no cottage here at all?"

"None's that anyone can use," the man said. "Abandoned place up around the next point – but nobody's been there for years. People owned it must have died, I think."

"You're sure there's been nobody there?"

"I'm sure. They'd have to cross my land to get to it, and I ain't seen nobody around here all week but you two kids. And what I can't see my dog smells – and she ain't said nothing about any stranger being around here."

"Can we walk further up?" Sarah asked.

"Long as you're careful," the farmer said. "Don't go near the cottage, though – it's a trap. Floor wouldn't hold you."

"We'll be careful," Travis said again.

The farmer nodded and moved back towards his field. They could see a large green tractor in the distance. He must have been taking off hay.

The dog stayed with them, dancing around them and splashing out into the water after imagined sticks. Travis was glad of the company.

Before long they rounded the next point.

"There it is!" Sarah said.

At first Travis couldn't see it, then gradually it came into focus: a black and grey, sun-bleached shack so old it seemed to blend in with the landscape. He could see broken windows, and a large tree branch that had fallen and caved in a portion of the roof.

"Let's get a closer look!" Sarah said.

"Okay," Travis said. He could hear the lack of confidence in his own voice, but Sarah was already splashing ahead, taking a shortcut through the shallows. Travis followed and expected the setter to splash ahead and catch up to Sarah, but there was no dog.

He turned. The setter was sitting there, whimpering, her tail wagging fast, her eyes filled with worry.

"What's wrong, girl?" Travis called.

Sarah stopped. "What's up?"

"The dog won't move."

Sarah shrugged. "Maybe she's trained to stay on her own property. Don't worry about her — she'll find her way back."

Travis stepped out into the water to join Sarah. It was cold against his bare legs and it tickled. The rocks were slimy. He slipped and nearly fell several times, but soon Travis and Sarah were almost to the broken-down dock that had once belonged to the cottage.

The dog was moaning. She was still sitting on the other side of the shallow bay, whining and wagging her tail hopefully.

"She's chicken!" said Travis.

"No way! Setters *love* water," Sarah said. "She's just trained not to wander, that's all."

"I guess," Travis said, but he wasn't so sure. Something was making him feel uneasy, too.

There was another moan, louder this time.

"Stupid dog," Travis said.

Sarah had stopped abruptly. "That wasn't the dog!" she whispered.

Travis felt a sharp chill run down his spine. He listened, and heard a low sorrowful groan from the cottage.

"I'm getting outta here!" he said.

"What if it's Joe Hall?" Sarah hissed.

"It can't be. The farmer never saw him. The dog would have known if someone was here."

Sarah pointed back to the setter, still watching, still fretting. "Maybe the dog *does* know," she said.

Travis felt his heart pound hard against his chest. He tried to speak, but his voice broke and creaked. "We're . . . not supposed to go in," he reminded Sarah.

"What if he needs help?"

"It's not even him," said Travis. "It's some animal. Maybe a skunk. Maybe even a *bear*."

"I'm going in," she said.

Sarah stepped up on shore. The dog on the far side of the water howled and barked. She began running back and forth frantically along the shore, but was afraid to come to them.

Sarah stepped cautiously along the dry, broken planks of the dock. Several were rotten and had turned to dust around the rusted nails. But she picked her way carefully, and Travis followed.

They could see where once there had been a path to the cottage. It was overgrown now and barely identifiable. Sarah pushed through, lowering her head against the flicking branches.

Travis was right behind her.

When she reached the cottage Sarah held up her hand for him to stop. The only sound was the frantic whining and barking of the setter in the distance.

"You hear anything?" Sarah asked.

"No," Travis said. He wanted to bolt. He wanted to run all the way back to his sleeping bag and jump into it and pretend that he'd never even heard of a cottage upstream from the camp.

Sarah stepped up onto the broken-down porch. A chipmunk scurried under, chattering wildly and frightening them both. But Sarah kept going. She came to the door and turned the latch. It swung open, surprisingly easily. Almost as if it had been recently oiled.

They stepped inside, Travis brushing aside cobwebs that clung to his hands like cotton candy. He almost gagged from the smell of must and rot.

Sarah stopped. She was shivering, uncertain where to head.

Travis didn't dare move.

Then he felt a large, cold, clammy hand settle on the back of his neck!

13

"WHAT ARE YOU TWO DOING HERE?"

The voice was familiar, though weak. Travis turned and stared up into the drawn, pale face of Joe Hall. He didn't look like "Bad" Joe Hall at all. He looked like "Sick" Joe Hall.

"We, we were looking for you," Travis admitted.

"Are you all right?" Sarah asked.

There was a long silence, then Joe Hall sighed. He seemed very tired.

"I'm fine," he said, unconvincingly. "You may as well go ahead in – but step carefully."

They edged past old furniture and even raspberry shoots that had pushed up inside the abandoned cottage. They passed through into a sitting room, where the light was falling in shafts through torn curtains.

There was a cot in the room. Joe Hall must have been lying there.

The light was better here, and the two Screech Owls took the opportunity to look more carefully at their new friend. Joe Hall looked terrible. His eyes seemed sunken and every few moments he shook from the inside out with a deep, quiet cough.

"You're sick!" Sarah said.

"It's just the flu," Joe Hall said. "I'll be fine for the game."

Sarah pushed aside the tattered curtains. The sun poured in through the broken and cob-webbed window, causing Joe Hall to blink and Sarah's and Travis's eyes to widen. He looked terrible. He'd lost weight.

"You need a doctor," said Sarah.

"I'll be fine," Joe Hall argued. "The worst is over."

"What're you doing here?" Travis asked.

"I come here sometimes," Joe Hall said. "No one knows about it. Place used to belong to the Westwick family. You remember I told you about Harry, the 'Rat'? I'm a bit of a student of 'Rat' Westwick, you might say." He smiled at Travis. "He's the one taught us that heel pass, remember?"

Travis nodded. He couldn't believe anyone would want to come here on their own. Especially if they were ill.

"If I'm the same after the big game," Joe Hall said, "I'll see a doctor. I promise you that, okay?"

He flashed his old smile and immediately looked much better. Sarah and Travis couldn't help themselves. They nodded, though they still felt he needed help now, not tomorrow. But Joe Hall wasn't going to listen to a couple of kids.

"You better head back to camp now," he said. "They'll be sending out a search party."

"I guess you're right," said Sarah. "You're sure you're going to be all right here, though?"

"I'm fine," Joe Hall said. He smiled again, but it wasn't so convincing this time. "I'll see you two at the rink, okay?"

They nodded in agreement.

Joe Hall walked them down to the dock, and when the setter caught sight of them it began to howl and moan. The dog seemed frantic, racing back and forth in the water, snapping and growling and barking.

"She's still waiting for us," Sarah said. "She wouldn't come across the water with us."

Joe Hall nodded, swallowed hard. "There's been a skunk around," he said. "I guess the dog smells it."

"I guess," Travis said.

The dog obviously had a better nose than he had. All Travis could smell was the musty old cottage and the river.

14

"*OH NO!*"

Travis had been first to break through the thick bush and find the path leading down into the camp. But when he did he saw that Nish's mad plan was already under way.

Fahd was waving frantically from near the flagpole. He was trying to catch Nish's attention. Nish was standing behind the boys' tent with Andy and Lars. Lars caught the signal and punched Nish's shoulder.

They peeked around the side of the tent just in time to see Sam leave the dining hall and head for the women's outhouse.

Nish broke across the camp at full speed, jumping from tree to bush to tree, as if no one would notice.

Sam went inside the outhouse and closed the door.

"What's going on?" Sarah asked from behind Travis.

"It's Nish's revenge," Travis said. "He's wired the outhouse for when Sam goes."

"'*Wired the outhouse*'?"

"He set some fireworks. He's going to fire them off when she's in there."

"That's *dangerous!*"

"Nish claims it's only a couple of big fire-crackers, and they're well below the seat in a wire cage."

"How'd he get down in there?"

"He won't say."

"He's insane."

"I know, I know."

Nish was now racing as fast as he could to the men's outhouse. Fahd already had the door open. Nish was in in a flash. Fahd shut the door and ran for the tent.

"What's happening?" Sarah asked.

"He's got this long fuse and he's going to light it from where he is."

"He knows what he's doing?"

"Nooo – but when has that ever stopped him?"

They waited. Sarah seemed apprehensive, worried about her friend. Travis was nervous as well, but worried also about his friend, Nish. He couldn't afford to get in any more trouble here.

There was a long pause. They could hear giggling coming from the direction of the boys' tent. Andy was making farting noises under his arm.

"How mature!" Sarah said.

They waited, but nothing happened. After a while the door to the women's outhouse opened and Sam came out. She walked right past Nish's hideout and washed her hands in the outside basin.

Still there was no explosion.

The boys had left the safety of their hideout behind the tent and were moving closer to the scene of the misfire.

"Nish?" Fahd called tentatively.

The door to the men's outhouse slipped open and a furious-looking Nish stepped out. He found the fuse on the ground and began tracing it along to the women's outhouse. He opened the door and slipped inside.

"What's that?" Sarah asked.

"Nish's fuse," Travis said. "It didn't work."

"No – what's *that*?" Sarah repeated.

She was pointing back to the men's outhouse. From the grass just outside came a small puff of smoke, followed by a little burst of light that sizzled and sparked and raced along the fuse right behind Nish.

Travis couldn't help himself: "*Nnniiiiiisshhhh!*"

KAAAAA-BOOOOOOMMMMMMMM!!!

KAAA-POWWWWWWW!

Travis had never seen anything like it. The women's outhouse seemed to jump about three feet in the air before crashing back down and wobbling from side to side. Smoke billowed from the air vent.

The door opened.

Out walked Nish, his arms straight down and his blinking eyes forming pink holes in the dark sludge that coated him from the top of this head to his sandals.

Nish was covered – completely, absolutely, and disgustingly – from head to foot *in human waste!*

"Very funny! *Very, very* funny!"

But it *was* very funny. No matter what Nish said. Sam laughed so loud and long she eventually pitched over onto her side and kicked her legs like she was riding an imaginary bike. Sarah laughed so hard she fell down on her knees. Fahd was crying he was laughing so hard. And Travis was laughing so hard he couldn't speak.

"*Stay still, you idiot!*" Mr. Dillinger shouted.

But even Mr. Dillinger was laughing. He was trying to be tough, but it wasn't working. Mr. Dillinger had a garden hose out and was standing a safe ten feet away from Nish and spraying him with the nozzle on full. Nish was turning, round and round and round, as the hose cut through the sludge and, slowly, a pink and highly embarrassed Wayne Nishikawa began to emerge.

When Mr. Dillinger had sprayed the worst parts with water, he shut off the hose and threw a bar of soap at Nish. "In the river, Mr. Manure," he said, fighting back a giggle. "You've got a good day of scrubbing ahead of you before anyone will even go near you."

Nish fumbled the soap, bent to pick it up, and slipped and fell, which only caused more laughter. He cradled the soap and began walking down towards the beach. When he reached the water he just kept on walking, almost as if he expected to walk across to the other side of the wide Ottawa River, but eventually he bobbed to the surface and began singing as he scrubbed.

He had obviously decided there was no use in fighting it. He may as well join in on the laughs.

"I do think he's insane, you know," Sarah said as she and Travis watched from the shore.

"He's different, that's for sure," said Travis.

"I think he's *neat!*"

Both Travis and Sarah turned at once.

It was Sam, flushing beneath her flaming red hair.

15

"HEY, DATA – HOW YA DOING?"

Data swivelled around in his chair. "Oh, hi, Travis. Nish all cleaned off yet?"

"It'll take him all summer – and even then he'll still smell like Nish."

Data laughed. He'd missed the explosion but had made it out in time to see Mr. Dillinger go to work with the hose. Data had been looking up *Star Wars* and *Star Trek* stuff on the Internet. The camp management had let him spend as much time on the camp computer as he wanted.

"What's up?" Data asked.

"I want you to find out something for me," Travis said.

"Shoot."

"I want to know more about Joe Hall."

"Get a grip, Travis – there's going to be about a million Joe Halls on the Web."

"But there's something different about this one. He used to play hockey. There's hundreds of hockey Web pages."

"And probably hundreds of Joe Halls who play or played hockey."

Travis was disappointed. The World Wide Web wasn't suddenly going to reveal all about Joe Hall. "I guess so," said Travis. "Thanks anyway."

Travis turned to go, but Data called him back.

"Don't give up so easily, Trav. What else do you know about him?"

"Nothing – that's the point. I wanted to see if there was *anything* I could find out."

"What do you suspect?"

"I don't know. Nothing, I guess."

"There must be something."

"I don't know, honestly. It's just that there's something not quite right about Joe Hall."

Data took a piece of paper and began scribbling. "'Joe Hall,'" he said. "Anything else?"

"I think he played at a high level, but I don't know when."

"What about a nickname?" Data asked.

"Yeah! 'Bad' Joe Hall. He told us."

"'Bad Joe Hall, hockey player,'" Data said. "I'll let you know."

"Thanks," Travis said. "Thanks for trying."

16

THE FINAL GAME OF THE LITTLE STANLEY CUP was set for Friday evening: Rideau Rebels versus the Screech Owls. It would be played at the Corel Centre and carried on The Sports Network. The Governor General was going to be there to present the Little Stanley Cup rings that had been made especially for the tournament. And the real, original Stanley Cup – the very one that Lord Stanley had been inspired to donate by the original Rideau Rebels – was going to be brought out of "retirement" and presented by the Governor General to the winning captain. Travis shuddered with excitement just imagining it.

But there was more. The original trophy had to be brought up from the Hockey Hall of Fame in Toronto, and the Hall was also going to put on a display at the Corel Centre featuring all the greats who had ever played for the original Cup, including Harry "Rat" Westwick and "One-Eyed" Frank McGee.

The excitement was getting to the whole team. Mr. Dillinger had sharpened everyone's skates so many times some of the Owls were deliberately "dulling" them by running the blades along the edge of an old hockey stick. Even Joe Hall seemed miraculously recovered. He was smiling again, that wonderful shining smile. And he looked freshly showered and shaved and was walking with a bounce.

"He's faking it," said Sarah. "Listen to him breathe."

When Joe Hall came up to Travis just before the warm-up, Travis immediately noticed that Sarah was right: his breathing was shallow, quick, and the quiet cough was still there.

"How about it today, Travis?" Joe Hall asked. "Try the stick?"

He seemed so hopeful, Travis had to think fast to come up with a way to please Joe Hall and, at the same time, get out of this predicament.

"I'll try it in the warm-up," he said.

"Go ahead," said Joe Hall. "It's all yours."

He got the stick for Travis. He seemed pleased. Travis put the stick to the side of his stall, not wanting anyone else to notice.

They entered the rink to pounding rock music and dazzling lights, brighter than they had ever seen. Of course, they were special lights for television, Travis realized. He instantly felt their heat.

But he was warm also from excitement. The crowd was enormous. There might be ten thousand people here, he thought. And there, in the special box to the right, was the Governor

General! She was waving to the crowd, and the people were applauding.

Everything felt wonderful to Travis – except the stick. It felt like a foreign object in his hands, something he had never held before.

He stickhandled a bit with it, then tried a shot. It rang off the crossbar – his good luck omen! Travis smiled to himself.

"*Where'd you get the goofy stick, jerk?*" a voice snarled in his ear.

It was Kenzie MacNeil, the big Rideau Rebels centre. He was laughing and pointing Travis out to his teammates.

"Is that some kind of joke?" James Grove asked.

"We'll see who's laughing at the end," Travis said. He sounded cocky, but he dumped the stick at the first opportunity and pulled out his Easton instead. He hoped Joe Hall wouldn't notice.

But he hoped in vain. Lining up for the opening faceoff, Travis glanced back at the bench. Joe Hall was staring right at him. He looked heartbroken.

It's not my fault, Travis thought. I never asked to use that stupid stick.

But there was no time to worry about it. The puck had dropped, the crowd exploded with noise, and the Rebels had possession.

Big MacNeil was turning in his own end. He seemed even larger this game, more assured of himself. He came up slowly, and Travis made his move to poke check.

Like a snake, MacNeil's stick moved back, tucking the puck away and then flipping it ahead, well out of Travis's reach. He was beaten. MacNeil moved down ice and ripped a hard slapper that Jeremy took on his pads.

Nish picked up the puck and cracked it off the boards back out to Travis. He cradled the puck, then began moving up ice. He faked a pass to Dmitri and instead fired the puck on his backhand off the near boards, neatly stepping around the player coming to check him. He was in three-on-one, with Sarah coming up fast.

Travis held the puck until the last moment, then tried to drop a pass to Sarah, but it rolled off the back of his curve and was lost.

He headed for the bench, anxious for a change. Joe Hall said nothing, but he didn't need to. Travis already blamed himself.

The game kept sailing end to end, but without a goal. Jeremy was fantastic, stealing goals from MacNeil twice with his glove, and once getting lucky with a shot that bounced away off the post. The Rebels' goalie was also hot. Twice he foiled Dmitri, and once he made a great blocker save on a hard drive by Nish from the point.

Nish was playing great. This was the Nish of championship games. He was all business, no nonsense. Perhaps Joe Hall had got through to him about his temper. Twice Joe Hall even paired him with Sam, and Nish kept his feelings, whatever they were, to himself. Perhaps he was still too embarrassed about the exploding outhouse to dare say anything to anyone.

The Rebels scored on a tip-in during a power play, and the Owls tied it up on a slick move by Simon Milliken when he was able to slip the puck over to a charging Andy for a hard backhand that beat the Rebels' goaltender. After one period it was 1–1, still 1–1 after two.

Late in the third period, with the score still tied, Travis chased MacNeil into the Rebels' corner. MacNeil stopped abruptly and turned so fast he ran over Travis, snapping Travis's stick as it fell between MacNeil's powerful legs.

Travis tossed his broken Easton away and made fast for the bench. Derek Dillinger saw him coming and leaped over the boards to replace him.

Data was already making his way to the rack to get Travis his second stick when, suddenly, Joe Hall grabbed Travis by the shoulder. Even through his shoulder pads and jersey he could feel the shake in Joe Hall's hand. He was very ill.

He looked up at his coach. Joe Hall's eyes were sunken again, but they held so much light they seemed to glow on their own. It had to be the television lights, Travis figured.

"Try mine," Joe Hall said.

Travis nodded. What choice did he have?

Joe Hall reached behind the bench and came up with his stick. Travis took it, reluctantly. It felt heavy, all wrong.

Travis looked up at the clock. Less than five minutes to go. At least he wouldn't have to use it for long.

But what if he had a chance and blew it? Would it be his fault – or Joe Hall's?

The Rebels almost scored with less than two minutes left when MacNeil broke in with his wingers and faked a shot that sent Sam to her knees and out of the play. He selfishly wound up for a hard slapshot and Nish threw himself in front of the shot, the hard drive glancing off his mask, then off the crossbar, before flying harmlessly over the glass.

Nish had saved the day.

He lay on the ice, not moving. Sam was already back on her feet and racing to him. She knelt down. Nish was blinking up, still stunned by the shot.

"That was sure no chicken play," she said, and smiled.

Nish got up slowly, feeling his helmet as if it might have been shattered. Sam gave him a grateful tap on the shinpads. The crowd applauded warmly. They knew they'd just seen a great defensive play.

"Great play, Nish!" Travis called as Nish came off the ice. "You saved a certain goal!"

Nish only nodded and sat to catch his breath. Travis didn't need to see his friend's face to know what colour it would be.

Travis took his first shift with Joe Hall's stick right after Nish's moment of glory. MacNeil was still out, and the Rebels' star pointed at Travis's old-style straight-as-a-ruler stick.

"The secret weapon?" MacNeil asked. His linemates laughed.

Travis rapped Joe Hall's stick hard on the ice. He wouldn't let them get to him.

The linesman held up his arm. The Owls were making one last change.

It was Nish – on with Sam – still shaking his head, but back to play.

Sarah won the faceoff. She pushed the puck to her left and bumped MacNeil out of the way.

Travis picked up the puck and immediately wished he had his Easton. The puck felt like lead. He stickhandled back and forth but worried he'd lose the puck.

He fired it back to Nish, who looped back into his own end. Slowly Nish went around the net, checking the time left – barely a minute – then doubled back again, unsure what to do.

Finally Nish fired the puck hard off the back-boards to Sam, who reversed direction and circled behind the net herself. She saw Travis free at the blueline and hit him with a perfect pass.

This time Travis didn't even try to stickhandle. He began, instead, to push the puck ahead of him and race down the side.

Travis's good speed gave him a jump on the Rebels' defence, and he made it to the blueline before his man turned on him.

Travis shot the puck across the ice to Dmitri. The lack of curve threw his aim off, and it flew ahead of Dmitri, who dashed into the corner to pick up the puck.

Dmitri made a beautiful move on his checker, passing to himself by backhanding the puck off the boards as the checker tried to take him out. He sidestepped the check, and the puck was instantly his again.

Dmitri hit Sarah coming in hard. She beat the one defence and backhanded the puck across to Travis.

Travis was afraid to shoot. He couldn't be sure he'd even hit the net. And the other defender was already on him, wrapping long arms around him.

The puck was loose in front of the two struggling players. Travis stared helplessly at it a second, then, without even thinking, hammered the back of the blade down hard on the edge of the puck.

The puck shot back between his legs – right back onto the stick of Sam, who was charging towards the net.

Travis clamped his arms down on the defender's arms. If he was going to be held, he'd hold, too. The defender couldn't move on Sam.

Sarah had the other defender out of position and pic-ed him so he couldn't get back in the play.

Sam faked once to her backhand, then blew right around the Rebels' goaltender and smacked the water bottle off the back of the net.

Owls 2, Rebels 1.

Fourteen seconds to play.

The players on the ice were all over Sam and Travis, but their teammates on the bench didn't dare jump over. With time still remaining, it would mean a penalty. But they were on their feet, stomping and yelling and high-fiving each other.

They lined up for the faceoff. MacNeil scowled at Travis, who held the stick blade up to his mask and pretended to kiss it. He felt like Nish doing it.

Sarah took the puck off MacNeil and shot it back to Sam, who dumped it back to Nish. The Rebels charged in desperation. Nish waited until the last moment before lobbing it out over everyone's head. Dmitri cuffed it at centre and the puck rolled into the Rebels' end, no offside, and big MacNeil, skating hard, barely got to it as the buzzer sounded.

The Screech Owls had won the Little Stanley Cup.

With "Bad" Joe Hall's heel pass.

17

THE CELEBRATION SEEMED TO GO ON FOREVER. The teams shook hands – "Great stick!" big MacNeil acknowledged with a good-hearted smile. The Governor General made her way down onto the ice for the presentation, and the ice filled with television cameras and radio and newspaper reporters asking for interviews, and photographers snapping shots of the Screech Owls as if they'd just won the Stanley Cup.

Which, of course, they had.

The first presentation, however, was to the Most Valuable Player. The public address system roared out the name – "SAMMM–ANTHA BENNNNN–ETTTTT!" – and Sam, standing down the line by Jenny Staples, threw off her helmet and shook her head as if she hadn't heard right.

But if Sam was surprised, no one else was. The crowd roared its approval and the Governor General handed her a beautiful little Inuit carving. Sam hugged the Governor General. Travis, hitting his stick on the ice, could only wonder if you were allowed to do that.

But the Governor General didn't seem to mind. She hugged Sam back. Then a large figure on skates stepped out of the Owls line and skated down to tap Sam's shinpads.

It was Nish, glowing like a goal light.

A moment later, a man wearing a dark blue suit and the whitest gloves Travis had ever seen came out from the Zamboni chute carrying the original Stanley Cup. It was so much smaller than the one Travis was familiar with from TV, but he knew that this one, the small one, was the *real* one. The same one that Lord Stanley had paid $48.67 for more than a century ago. Today, it was priceless.

The Owls and Rebels lined up and the Governor General presented the Rebels with silver medals, which she placed around their necks. The Owls raised their sticks in salute and cheered the home-town team.

Travis turned to Sarah. "Find Joe," he said. "And fast."

Sarah skated away.

The Governor General then picked up the original Stanley Cup. She looked around for the team captain.

"Go, Trav!" Nish called, hammering his stick.

"Yeah, Travis!" Sam shouted.

Travis noticed Sam and Nish were now standing side by side. Something seemed to have changed between them.

But he wasn't looking for Sam or Nish. He had to find Joe Hall.

The Governor General was walking towards Travis with the Stanley Cup in her hands. The Rebels were pounding their sticks on the ice in salute. The entire Corel Centre was on its feet, cheering.

Travis looked around, nearly frantic.

There was Sarah! And she had Joe Hall with her.

Joe Hall, white as the ice, was leaning heavily on Sarah. He looked terrible.

Travis turned first to Joe Hall. He handed him back his stick. The sparkle was missing, but Joe Hall managed a thin, quick smile.

"You won the Stanley Cup for me," he said.

Then the Governor General presented the Stanley Cup to Travis. With trembling arms he took the trophy, thanked her, and raised it over his head to thunderous cheers.

Travis knew that everyone expected him to hand the Cup next to his assistant captain, Sarah. But Sarah stepped aside, and Travis, smiling, did what both of them knew needed to be done. He handed the original Stanley Cup to Joe Hall.

Joe Hall reached for it. He was crying. Sobbing openly, huge tears welled up in his eyes and rolled down his cheeks, splashing into the Stanley Cup.

"Thanks, Joe," Travis said. "And congratulations."

Sarah reached up and kissed Joe Hall. Still sobbing, he handed the trophy to Sarah. Sarah lifted it, then handed it off to Derek, then Nish.

Nish pushed past several of the Owls to make sure Sam got it next. She raised the cup and did a little dance, much to the delight of the crowd.

18

"WHERE DID JOE HALL GO?" ASKED TRAVIS.

Sarah looked around. "I hope he's gone to see a doctor."

Travis had no time to go look for him. There were photographers and reporters and more cheers and a Little Stanley Cup ring to try on. Soon an hour or more had passed, and they still hadn't seen Joe Hall.

Finally, with the cheering over and the ice already being cleaned, the triumphant Owls made their way back to the dressing room. Mr. Dillinger was there, packing up the equipment for the long bus ride home.

But still no Joe Hall.

Travis undressed, showered, and changed. He was just doing up his shirt when Data wheeled up and handed him a folded piece of paper. "You might want to look at this, Travis."

It was, as Travis expected, the results of Data's computer search for Joe Hall. Sure enough, it turned out there were hundreds of Joe Halls, even several Joe Halls in hockey. But only one "Bad" Joe Hall.

Travis read frantically.

Hall, Joe: "Bad" Joe Hall was born in England but was raised in Canada. He played professional hockey at the beginning of the 20th Century, mostly for the Montreal Canadiens. He was famous for his bad temper – he was once taken off the ice in a police paddy wagon! – but later came to regret the playing time his temper had cost him. Hall's Canadiens met the Seattle Metropolitans to decide the 1919 Stanley Cup, but the Spanish flu struck the Montreal team badly. Five players were too sick to play, and when Joe Hall died, the championship was cancelled that year – the only time in history there has been no Stanley Cup awarded.

Travis read it twice. He could make no sense of it. *It was impossible.*

Sarah popped her head into the dressing room.

Travis looked up, hopeful. "Did you find him?"

Sarah shook her head, then she stopped and smiled. "I don't know – maybe I did."

Travis was more puzzled than ever. Either she had found Joe Hall or she hadn't.

"Come on out here a minute," Sarah said.

She took him up the back stairs to the front foyer of the Corel Centre, where the original Stanley Cup was back on display and the fans were lining up by the hundreds to have their pic-tures taken with it and the other trophies from the Hockey Hall of Fame.

But it wasn't the trophies that Sarah wanted to show him. "Over here," she said. "The display cases."

They moved over to several large glass cases containing memorabilia from the Silver Seven and the early Ottawa Senators. There were even photographs of the Rideau Rebels, and a great picture of "One-Eyed" Frank McGee and Harry "Rat" Westwick.

But she wanted to show him something else. "Look in this case," Sarah said.

Travis peered in. Old skates, equipment, sweaters, a hockey stick. He saw nothing to tell him where Joe Hall had gone.

"What?" he said.

"Recognize the stick?" she asked.

Travis looked again. It was in the far corner of the case. An old, perfectly straight hockey stick.

And at the top, near the handle, was pencilled a single name.

"J. Hall."

THE END

The West Coast Murders

It was Sarah who spotted the first body . . .

The Screech Owls' journey to Vancouver had begun as an innocent hockey road trip. They had come to play in the new "three-on-three" shinny tournament. But when the team headed out to sea to watch the first whales of the season return to the West Coast, the dream trip turned into a horrifying adventure.

It was Travis who spotted the second one . . .

Two bodies – one a dolphin, one a man – bobbing in the tide. And when Nish stared down at the floating, twisting body of the man and announced "We know him!" the Screech Owls also knew they were in the middle of a baffling mystery.

Slowly, the truth begins to emerge: a diabolical smuggling operation, a heroic dolphin, mad scientists, and a wildly brilliant plan. The Screech Owls are almost enjoying themselves, until they discover their own lives are in danger!

THE SCREECH OWLS SERIES